Main Street

September Surprises

Main Street

September Surprises

Ann M. Martin

SCHOLASTIC INC.

NEW YORK   ND ◇ SYDNEY
MEXICO CITY ◇ NEW DELHI ◇ HONG KONG ◇ BUENOS AIRES

ISBN-13: 978-0-439-86884-6
ISBN-10: 0-439-86884-X

Illustrations by Dan Andreason

12 11 10 9 8 7 6 5 4 3 2 1   8 9 10 11 12 13/0

Printed in the U.S.A.   23

First printing, September 2008

Main Street

September Surprises

Camden Falls

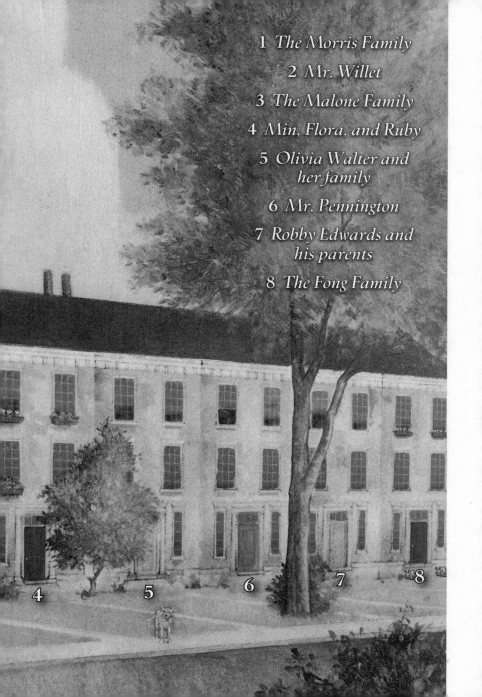

4   5   6   7   8

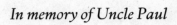

In memory of Uncle Paul

CHAPTER I

A Peek in the Windows

If you have never been to Camden Falls, Massachusetts, you might feel a small thrill, a little shiver up your back, the first time you see one of the signs reading WELCOME TO CAMDEN FALLS. There are four of these signs on the outskirts of town — one on the approach from the county road near where Nikki Sherman lives, one several miles out on Boiceville Road, and two on Route 6A, one facing north and one facing south. The people who live in Camden Falls take little notice of the signs. They pass them often, and the signs have become part of the landscape of their lives, like trees and rock walls and their own driveways — comfortable and comforting, but unremarkable.

If you are a newcomer to Camden Falls, though, consulting your map and following directions as the road unfurls before you, you might feel a surge of relief

1

and excitement when at last you see one of the signs. Fourteen months ago, two sisters, Flora and Ruby Northrop, saw the north-facing sign and knew their lives were about to change forever. The girls felt neither relief nor excitement and tried hard not to cry. But on this late August day, a man driving along Route 6A comes to one of the signs and begins to smile. It's not the first time he's seen the sign, but it's one of the first times, and the experience still makes his heart sing. He's ready for a new phase of his life, ready to settle down in this small town where everybody knows everybody, or at least almost everybody. In Camden Falls, he imagines, you can walk along Main Street and greet the shopkeepers and appreciate the changes, great and small, that each season brings.

This newcomer hasn't yet met his neighbors, hasn't experienced Halloween on Main Street, hasn't seen the field of pumpkins at Davidson's Orchards, isn't acquainted with Min and Gigi and Mrs. Grindle and the Walters and the other Main Street shopkeepers, and doesn't know that Flora Northrop (now a different and much happier girl) will be one of his memorable seventh-grade pupils at Camden Falls Central High School this year. Still, the sign makes him smile, and he relaxes as he turns right off of 6A, then right again onto Main Street, and finally through town to his new home, pleased with himself for already knowing the route.

This man — Vincent Barnes is his name — steers his car confidently toward his new house and his new life. Leave him for now and take a closer look at Main Street. If you stand with your back to Stuff 'n' Nonsense, you'll see Needle and Thread, Camden Falls's sewing store, across the street. It's the end of the day and Min and Gigi, co-owners of the store and grandmothers to Flora and Ruby Northrop and Olivia Walter, are closing up shop. Min looks at her watch, then out the window, and remarks, "The days are already growing shorter. Have you noticed? Not Labor Day yet, but fall is on the way."

Turn right and walk to the end of the block. Kitty-corner across the street are the neon lights spelling out MARQUIS DINER. The signs of the fire that destroyed the building at the beginning of the summer are barely visible, and the diner will re-open shortly. The Nelsons, the family who owns the Marquis, are locking the door and leaving for their rented home. "If," says ten-year-old Hilary Nelson, "there had never been a fire, we wouldn't have to go anywhere when it was time to close up. We'd already be at home." She looks wistfully at the apartment above the diner that was destroyed along with the Marquis. It's been a difficult summer for Hilary and her family.

Now turn left on Dodds Lane, then right on Aiken Avenue. The long stone building ahead of you is home to Min, Flora, and Ruby, to Olivia Walter and her family, and to six other families. Eight tidy yards, eight front doors — these are the Row Houses, and the people who live here make up a small community of their own. A peek in the windows shows you that it's nearly supper time for most of these families. In the house on the left end, the Morris children are helping their parents by setting the table. Mr. Morris is stirring spaghetti sauce, Mrs. Morris is chopping vegetables for a salad, Travis is saying, "Can we eat dinner outside?" and Alyssa, the youngest Morris, is saying, "When I start kindergarten, can I have a new bedtime?"

Next door to the Morrises is the quietest house in the row. It's the home of Mr. and Mrs. Willet, but earlier this year, Mrs. Willet moved into a nursing home, and Mr. Willet, married to his beloved Mary Lou for decades and decades, has decided to join her there. He can't bear to be alone any longer. Now he's standing in front of the freezer, trying to decide which frozen meal to heat up for his dinner. His cat, Sweetie, sits on the counter, watching him.

At the other end of the row, Mr. and Mrs. Fong are feeding their baby and their dogs and making their own dinner at the same time. "Bedlam," says Barbara Fong, looking fondly around the kitchen, although it really isn't bedlam at all.

In the middle two houses live Flora and her family and Olivia and her family. Min is still closing up

Needle and Thread, but Flora and Ruby, in the fourth house from the left, have gotten supper underway on their own.

"We're almost like real cooks," says Ruby, who's ten. "I wish I had a chef's hat."

"Min's going to be surprised by dessert," replies Flora. "She doesn't know we learned how to make brownies."

Flora and Ruby have only recently been allowed to use the stove when Min isn't home, and they are proud of themselves.

Next door, in the fourth house from the right, Olivia and her mother stand side by side in the kitchen, while in the living room, Olivia's brothers fight over the remote control for the television. "Do you ever get tired of cooking?" Olivia asks her mother. Her parents own a store on Main Street called Sincerely Yours. Among the items for sale are candies and baked goods made by Mrs. Walter.

Mrs. Walter pauses. "It's my passion," she replies.

Olivia nods. She understands passions. But she isn't sure her friends understand *her* passion, which is science. "Mom," says Olivia, "I don't want to go to the central school."

Mrs. Walter considers her daughter. "I know you don't. But your dad and I are here to help you. Always remember that."

In every corner of Camden Falls, stories are

unfolding. Peek in the windows of houses, of stores, of businesses, of workshops, and you'll find drama and ordinariness and life marching forward. Here is Mr. Barnes unlocking the door to his new home. Here is Alyssa Morris waiting impatiently for kindergarten to begin. Here is Mr. Willet poised to leave the Row Houses. And here are Flora and Ruby Northrop, Olivia Walter, and Nikki Sherman — best friends — at the end of another summer with a new school year stretching ahead. They are about to turn the corner to September, leaving August behind.

CHAPTER 2

Monday, September 1ˢᵗ

Flora Northrop paid close attention to the passage of time. She enjoyed counting things. In June, she had counted the days of summer vacation that lay ahead (seventy-five). She liked knowing how many days until her birthday and until Christmas. One year, she had begun counting the days to her birthday on the day after her previous birthday, and so all year long she woke up thinking, Three hundred and sixty-four days. Or, A hundred and eighty-three days. Not until she reached fifty did she start adding the word *just* at the beginning of each thought: Just fifty more days. Just seventeen more days. And at long last, Just one more day until my birthday!

On Labor Day, September 1ˢᵗ of the year in which Flora would move to the big central school and begin seventh grade there, she found herself doing quite a lot of counting. Only one more day of summer vacation, was her first thought of the morning. She was still lying in her bed, and when she peeked over the edge, she found Daisy Dear sprawled on the floor below, looking hopefully up at Flora, her golden tail sweeping the floor. Flora reached down and rubbed Daisy's belly.

"Can you believe that Ruby and I have lived here with you for . . ." (Flora closed her eyes and thought) "for fourteen months," she said after a moment, "and I'm not sure how many days. Seven or eight, maybe. *Can* you believe it, Daisy? I can't. And tomorrow school starts. Then nine and a half months of school —"

"Are you talking to yourself again?" called Ruby from her bedroom across the hall.

"Sort of," said Flora.

"Either you are or you aren't."

"I am."

"I bet you're counting stuff, too," said Ruby. "Starting with days left of vacation. And ha-ha, I have *three* more days."

Flora didn't reply. She trailed her hand up and down Daisy's furry tummy and wished dogs could purr.

"Flora?" said Ruby.

"*Shh.* I need my thinking time."

"Okay. But you don't want to be late for Nelson Day. If today *does* have to be your last one of vacation —

your last one, not mine, ha-ha — at least it'll be a pretty good day."

"I know. But I still need my thinking time."

No further sounds issued from Ruby's room. Flora returned to her thoughts. She wondered if maybe tomorrow couldn't be considered a vacation day as well. Or at least not a school day, since it wasn't officially the first day of school. What it was, officially, was orientation for the seventh-graders at Camden Falls Central High School, the huge school that served all the students in grades seven through twelve from Camden Falls and six surrounding townships.

No wonder we need orienting, Flora thought. Not only was the school unfamiliar (and giant), but most of the students would be unfamiliar, too. The only ones Flora would know were those who had been with her in the sixth-grade classes at Camden Falls Elementary, the school Ruby would have the good fortune to attend for two more years.

Flora felt a surge of panic. It rose from her belly into her chest. "Come up here with me, Daisy," she said desperately, and she patted her blankets and coaxed the galumphing golden retriever until at last Daisy heaved herself onto Flora's bed. A bit reluctantly, Flora thought. Still, it was pleasant and very comforting to be able to fling her arms around Daisy Dear and hold tight, something she hadn't been able to do before she and Ruby had moved to Camden Falls to live with Min. Daisy was Min's dog, and before the momentous change in Flora's life, Flora had known only cats — a trail of them, ending with King Comma, who now lived under Min's roof as well and, to Flora's relief, had made his peace with the idea of sharing close quarters with a dog.

The momentous change in Flora's life had taken place nineteen and a half months earlier, on a bitterly cold and stormy January night. A truck traveling too fast on a slick road had collided with the car in which Flora was riding with Ruby and their parents. Flora and Ruby had survived, unhurt; their parents had been killed instantly. And just like that, Flora's life had changed. Oh, she knew that her life — that everybody's lives — changed every single second of every single day. But there was no denying that some changes were bigger than others, and had much bigger consequences. The accident was one of them. Flora thought, in fact, that there was a good chance no bigger change would ever happen to her or to Ruby.

After the accident, Min had temporarily left behind her life in Camden Falls and had gone to stay with Flora and Ruby in their home. But by the end of the school year, she had sold their house, packed up their belongings, and moved her granddaughters back to Camden Falls — to the row house in which not only Min had grown up, but Flora and Ruby's own mother as well.

Flora, who had thought she would live in her hometown until she went to college, now found herself in a different town — in a different bedroom in a different house with different best friends and a very different life.

"Flora? Are you done thinking?" called Ruby.

"I guess."

"Well, come on, then. We don't want to miss a second of Nelson Day. Min's going to leave soon."

Flora looked at Daisy. "You can go now," she told her. "I know you want to." Daisy leaped off the bed and skittered out of the room, and Flora closed her door so she could have privacy while dressing.

From the hallway she heard Ruby's voice again. "Is Olivia coming with us or is she going to meet us in town?"

"She's meeting us in town. Nikki, too," Flora called.

"I hope Nelson Day raises lots and lots of money for Hilary's family," said Ruby. "And to think it was all my idea."

Flora, fully dressed, opened her door. "At least you're modest about it," she said.

"Girls?" Min's voice floated up from the first floor. "Are you coming with me? I need to leave for the store in twenty minutes."

"Coming!" Flora and Ruby dashed down the stairs and into the kitchen. They ate a hurried breakfast while Min drank one final cup of coffee.

"You should see the corduroy that came in on Friday," Min remarked. "Some really lovely florals and paisleys."

Ruby, who had no interest whatsoever in corduroy or fabric or sewing, said nothing. But Flora looked eagerly at her grandmother. "Really? Could I make something for one of the store displays? A vest, maybe?"

"Hey, could we decorate the window for Halloween?" said Ruby, without waiting for Min to answer Flora. She remembered with sudden happiness the hours she, her sister, Nikki, and Olivia had spent decorating the window of Needle and Thread for Christmas the previous year.

"Yes to both of you," replied Min.

"Thank you," said Flora.

"Sweet!" said Ruby.

"Ready?" asked Min. And she and her grand-daughters set out for Main Street and Nelson Day and the last bits of summer vacation.

CHAPTER 3

Tuesday, September 2ⁿᵈ

"It's over, it's over," moaned Olivia, as she slid into her place at the breakfast table.

"What? Vacation?" asked her brother Henry with a smirk. He grinned across the table at Jack. "Not for us. We still have two more days."

"No. Not vacation," replied Olivia, making a face. "My life."

"*Oliv*ia," said her mother. "For heaven's sake."

Olivia slid her plate aside and buried her head in her arms. "Well, it is. The central school is too big. And I'll probably be the youngest student there. Everyone is going to tease me. Only now there'll be a million more kids to do the teasing. Why did I ever have to skip a grade?"

"I'm sorry you're so smart," said her father.

"And what kind of an attitude is that?" asked her mother.

"A pitiful one," mumbled Olivia. "But I don't care."

"Well, if you go off to school in this frame of mind," said Mr. Walter, "you're bound to have a bad day. No matter what happens."

Olivia said nothing.

"How long does orientation last?" asked her father more gently.

"I think it's over at eleven."

"Why don't you come to the store afterward and tell us all about it? Bring Flora and Nikki with you, if you want. We'll buy sandwiches at the market and you girls can have a picnic at the store."

"Hey, why do they get a treat?" asked Jack, dropping his spoon indignantly into his cereal, causing a splash.

"Everyone gets treats at different times for different reasons," said Mrs. Walter evenly. "Now, come on, Olivia. I insist you eat breakfast before you leave. No skipping meals."

"Maybe that's why she's so small for her age," murmured Henry. "Maybe —" But he was silenced by a look from his parents.

Wordlessly, Olivia ate her breakfast, then dropped a pad of paper into her backpack, in case she needed to take notes. As she headed for the front door, she said over her shoulder to her family, "This may be one of the last times you see me alive. I've heard what the older kids at Central do to the seventh-graders on the first day of school. So you all better enjoy me today. I might not survive tomorrow."

She slammed the door behind her and didn't hear Jack's startled question: "*What* do the big kids do on the first day of school, Mommy?"

Olivia crossed her yard and trudged up Flora's front steps. She was about to ring the bell when the door opened and out stepped Flora, her own backpack slung over one shoulder.

"Good luck, girls!" called Min from the kitchen. "Flora, stop in at the store on your way home, okay?"

"Hey, my dad said to come to Sincerely Yours for —" Olivia started to say, but she stopped when a window above her was flung open.

"Have fun at school, ha-ha!" Ruby shouted from her bedroom. "I'll just be up here, playing on the computer and —"

"Ruby!" called Min from somewhere inside the house. "Get dressed now, please. You have to come to the store with me this morning. You can't stay here alone."

"Dang," Ruby said loudly, and closed the window.

Olivia looked at Flora and they began to laugh. But Olivia's smile faded quickly. "Are you nervous?" she asked.

Flora nodded. "Definitely."

The girls walked to the end of the block, but where they would have turned right to go to the elementary school, they now turned left toward Main Street.

"It'll be kind of fun to walk right down Main Street every morning, won't it?" asked Flora. "That's one reason I didn't sign up to take the bus to Central, even if it is kind of a long walk."

"Well, I'm afraid of the bus, but . . . I liked walking to our old school. I did it for seven years."

"Maybe it's time for a change."

"I don't like change."

Flora sighed. She didn't particularly like change either.

Olivia stared stolidly ahead as she and Flora marched past Needle and Thread, past Sincerely Yours, past all the familiar landmarks of town, and then made a left and a right and at last . . .

"There it is," whispered Olivia. Camden Falls Central High School loomed ahead of them. "It looks like a fortress or a castle. A castle with gallows."

"At least today only the seventh-graders will be here."

"No. The older kids are going to show us around," said Olivia.

"Well, I'm sure the teachers didn't ask rude, mean kids to do that job."

"Even nice kids might want to play tricks on us."

"Olivia! Stop!" cried Flora. "You're making this worse. Look. There's Nikki. Come on. Nikki! Hi!"

Nikki Sherman had been standing uncertainly near the spot where her bus had let her off. Now she turned, saw Olivia and Flora, and dashed toward them.

"You guys!" she exclaimed. "I've been watching everyone go in the building, and I don't know a single soul except for the kids who were on the bus." Nikki glanced apprehensively toward the open double doors through which a stream of seventh-graders was passing.

"Everyone looks as nervous as we do," remarked Flora.

Olivia, Flora, and Nikki joined the kids, and moments later, Olivia found herself in a wide hallway lined with glass cases containing school trophies and photos of Central's sports teams. Two girls who, Olivia thought, must be at least sixteen years old (they had chests, actual chests), were smiling and holding up a sign reading THIS WAY TO AUDITORIUM.

"They look friendly," Nikki whispered, but as Olivia walked by them, one of the girls touched her shoulder and said, "Are you supposed to be here? No visitors. Orientation is for seventh-graders only."

"I *am* in seventh grade," said Olivia, feeling her face grow hot. "I'm just not twelve yet." She stalked down the hall ahead of her friends, thinking, And I'm skinny and I'm short and I look like I'm about nine.

"Olivia, she wasn't being mean," called Nikki,

hurrying to catch up with her. "Honest. She was just doing her job."

"That. Doesn't. Make it. Any. Better."

That morning, Olivia tried to pay attention. She sat in the auditorium (which was, she thought, at least twice as big as the auditorium at her old school) and appeared to listen while the principal made a speech. But by the end of the speech, she couldn't remember a word he'd said. She had, however, spotted Tanya Rhodes and Melody Becker sitting two rows ahead of her. Why, thought Olivia, did *they* have to be the first of the very few kids she actually recognized? Tanya and Melody, two of the most popular girls in her sixth-grade class at Camden Falls Elementary, had never been particularly nice to Olivia, not even after she had given an end-of-the-summer party a few days ago and invited them to it. (Tanya had shown up without bothering to RSVP, and neither Tanya nor Melody had given Olivia the time of day — at her *own* party at which *she* was the hostess.) As Olivia watched them, they turned around, caught sight of Flora and Nikki, waved to them, and then passed over Olivia as they continued to scan the auditorium. Olivia slumped. The day was going just as she had feared it would.

The speech over, the students were directed to the gym, where they were handed their schedules for the semester. Then they were divided into groups and given a tour of the school. Olivia, separated from Nikki and Flora, followed meekly at the back of her group, up and down staircases, along hallways, around corners, in and out of wings, until at last she truly had no idea where she was.

At eleven o'clock, her guide, a pleasant enough sophomore who introduced himself as Ray, deposited Olivia and the other students on the front lawn of Central and said, "Well, if there are no more questions, I'll see you tomorrow. Good luck finding your way around."

Olivia cast desperately about for her friends. When at last she spotted them, they ran to her, and Nikki actually hugged her. "I have absolutely no idea where anything is in there," she said, pointing over her shoulder to the school.

Olivia would have laughed if she hadn't felt exactly the same way. "I feel *dis*oriented," she said. "They should rename this day."

"I don't even know where my *first* class is," moaned Flora. "What am I going to do tomorrow morning? I need a map."

"Pull out a map and everyone will *know* you're in seventh grade," said Nikki.

Olivia sighed. "Well, come on. Nikki, my dad promised us a picnic at the store. Let's go." She threw one final terrified look at Camden Falls Central High School, then linked arms with Nikki and Flora and headed for Main Street.

Orientation was over.

CHAPTER 4

Wednesday, September 3rd

"Nikki, is it true your new school is as big as a castle?" Mae Sherman asked her sister.

Nikki smiled. "No. That's just what Olivia said. She was exaggerating. And anyway, my new school is Tobias's old school. You know what it looks like."

"*Oh*. Tobias's *old* school." Mae nodded sagely, wearing her wise owl look. "You go to Tobias's old school, and now I'm the only one in our family going to Camden Falls Elementary."

"That's right. But today," said Nikki, sitting up in bed and trying to ignore the butterflies in her stomach, "you have one more day at day care before you start second grade. Is your class going to do anything special?"

Mae yawned. "We're going to the dollar store."

"What? Seriously?"

"Yes. We'll each have two dollars to spend. We're supposed to see how many things we can buy."

"Well, won't everybody get two things?"

Mae gave Nikki a look of disgust. "*Some* things," she said, "cost *less* than a dollar. So it's a" (she paused) "a challenge. And we use our math skills."

"Buy me something special," said Nikki, and Mae laughed. "Come on. Time to get dressed."

In a flash, Mae threw on a pair of shorts, a pink shirt, and her sneakers. Nikki lingered in front of her closet. In the last four days she had chosen five outfits for the first day of seventh grade. Each had been the final choice, and then she had reconsidered it and changed her mind. The fifth choice was now lying over the back of Nikki's desk chair.

"I can't wear that," she said aloud.

"Why not?" asked Mae, tying her sneakers.

"It looks — I just can't — I don't know."

Nikki grabbed a pair of jeans and a white shirt from her bureau drawer, muttered, "These'll be fine," and put them on without bothering to glance in the mirror. She didn't have time to change her mind again.

Mae ran ahead of her sister, down the stairs to the kitchen. But Nikki paused outside the door to Tobias's bedroom. Her brother had telephoned the night before, and as Nikki stared around his bare room, she remembered their conversation. Her mother had answered the phone and motioned for Nikki and Mae to get on the extension.

"Hi!" Mae had squealed.

"Hi, everyone," Tobias had replied, already sounding, Nikki thought, miles more sophisticated than when he had called two days earlier to say he had arrived safe and sound at college. Tobias was the first Sherman to go to college, and Nikki was in awe of him. College, she felt, must be terribly exciting. Glamorous, even. Tobias had roommates. He had his own computer. He was taking courses with names like Environmental Politics, Communication, and Intro to Psychology.

"How are you girls doing?" he'd asked, after he had answered Nikki's many questions about his dorm and his roommates.

"Fine, we're fine," Mrs. Sherman assured him.

"Really? No phone calls or visitors?"

This was Tobias's way of making sure, without frightening Mae, that Mr. Sherman hadn't been in touch with his family.

"We've gotten about three million phone calls from Olivia and Flora," said Mae. "Did you know, Tobias, that in seventh grade you lose your head?"

"What?" said Tobias.

"What?" said Nikki and Mrs. Sherman.

"It's true. Nikki can't decide what to wear to school tomorrow and neither can Flora or Olivia, and first Nikki says she wants to go to Central and then she says she doesn't, and first she says she's scared to ride the new bus and then she says —"

Tobias had laughed. "Okay, I get it."

"Nikki!" Mrs. Sherman now called from downstairs, and Nikki shook her head. She left Tobias's room and the memory of his phone call behind her, and dashed to the kitchen. Half an hour later, she was running down the lane to the county road, in such a hurry to make her bus that she couldn't even worry about the fact that the next morning, Mae would face the elementary school bus without her big sister to watch out for her. Or that in forty-five minutes, her own bus would deposit her in front of Central and seventh grade would begin in earnest.

She reached the end of her lane just as the bus appeared at the top of a little rise on the road. The bus groaned to a stop, and Nikki drew in her breath, stepped aboard, looked at the rows of faces (now including those of kids much older than she), and let out her breath again. The other students barely glanced at her. Some were dozing, some were bent over their cell phones, and two who were old friends of Tobias's gave her sleepy waves. Gone were the smirking ten-year-olds holding their noses as she and Mae walked by. Gone were the tripping feet, the poking fingers. Maybe there was an advantage to being with older students, thought Nikki.

When the bus doors opened for the last time and

the kids filed off the bus, Nikki felt a surge of confidence. Central rose ahead of her, now looking more like a school and less like a fortress. She saw Flora and Olivia waiting exactly where she had met them the day before.

"Ready?" she asked.

"Ready," Flora replied.

"I hope so," Olivia said.

The day began. At first Nikki tensed, expecting with each turn of a corner to encounter an older student who would back her against the lockers or direct her to perform some odious task. But absolutely nothing out of the ordinary happened. Nikki and Flora and Olivia easily found their way to the junior high wing, and Nikki got lost only twice that morning and both times was helped by a teacher. She liked her classes, and she realized in the very first one that the rest of the students felt just as apprehensive as she did. Why had that not occurred to her earlier? This was a new school for everyone in her entire grade.

At lunchtime, Nikki, Olivia, and Flora once again managed to locate one another. They sat at the end of a table separated by four empty spaces from the other students, who were either seventh-graders or tenth-graders (two grades sharing each of the three lunch periods), and ate the food they purchased in the cafeteria.

"The food's better here," ventured Olivia in a small voice.

"More choices," Nikki agreed.

"But it's an awfully big room," said Flora, gazing around at the crowded, noisy tables.

"I think that's Claudette Tisch over there," said Nikki. "See? Sitting with Mary Louise Detwiler?"

"Should we go sit with them?" asked Olivia.

"No. I'm happy right here," replied Nikki. And she *was* happy. Happy in the tiny, safe world formed by her two best friends. The day was going fine, just fine, so far. She didn't want to do anything to jinx it. Maybe tomorrow or the next day they could expand their horizons. But not yet.

CHAPTER 5

Thursday, September 4ᵗʰ

There was a nip in the air on Ruby Northrop's first day of school. That was what Min called the chilly weather that had arrived overnight.

"You two better wear sweaters," she said as she and Ruby and Flora were finishing their breakfast.

"But I don't —" Ruby began to protest.

"*Or* jackets or sweatshirts," finished Min. "I insist, Ruby. The thermometer says fifty-two this morning."

Ruby suppressed the urge to reply, "Our thermometer talks?"

"It *is* cold, Ruby," spoke up Flora, who had draped a windbreaker over the back of her chair. "I got goose bumps when I walked Daisy."

"All *right*," muttered Ruby. "I'll put on a stupid sweatshirt."

"Will you also put on a smile, please?" asked Min. "I

don't want you walking out the door and off to the first day of school with that attitude. What will Mrs. Caldwell think? I'd like your new teacher to meet Pleasant Ruby, not Crabby Ruby."

Ruby considered the request. Was it worth a fight? She decided it wasn't. She was actually looking forward to fifth grade. She just hadn't wanted to get up so early.

Flora stood then, carried her dishes to the sink, grabbed the windbreaker, and hurried into the hallway, where she hefted her backpack. "Bye!" she called. "See you this afternoon. I'll stop in at the store, Min."

"Wait!" cried Ruby. "Don't you want to watch me leave?"

"Oh, is there going to be some kind of show?" asked Flora sweetly.

Ruby opened her mouth to protest, but Min said quickly, "Girls, for pity's sake, what has gotten into you? Flora, go meet Olivia. Ruby, I'll watch you leave."

Min wasn't the only Row House adult standing on her stoop that morning, watching the elementary students begin the new school year. At the north end of the row, the Fongs were outside, Mr. Fong holding Grace aloft and saying to her, "See all the big kids? In five years we'll be watching *you* leave for kindergarten."

Next door to the Fongs, Mr. and Mrs. Edwards and Robby were sitting in a row on their stoop. This was the first year that Robby, who was eighteen and had Down syndrome, hadn't gone off to school himself. "I used to be one of them, didn't I? Didn't I, Mom and Dad? I used to be one of them. But I like my job."

Mr. Pennington left his house and joined Min at hers, waving to the Walters as he crossed their yard. Next door to Min, Dr. Malone was at his screen door, a cup of coffee in his hands. His teenage daughters, Lydia and Margaret, had already left for Central, but the sight of the younger children made him remember the years when he would stand on the stoop with his wife and watch Lydia and Margaret, their hair in ponytails, hands clutching lunch boxes, run down Aiken Avenue toward the elementary school. Next door to Dr. Malone stood Mr. Willet, thinking that this was the last time he would participate in this September Row House ritual.

At the house on the south end of the row, Mr. and Mrs. Morris held open their door as all four of their children filed out of it.

"Have fun!" called Mr. Morris.

"Lacey or Mathias, one of you be sure to hold Alyssa's hand when you cross the street," said Mrs. Morris. "Alyssa, remember, I'll pick you up at your classroom at lunchtime, okay?"

"Yes, yes, yes!" sang Alyssa.

Ruby joined the group of Row House children walking to CFE — Jack and Henry Walter, and Lacey, Mathias, Travis, and Alyssa Morris — and set off for her first day of school.

When the kids reached Camden Falls Elementary, Ruby called good-bye to Lacey and skipped off to the fifth-grade classrooms. She reached Mrs. Caldwell's, marched inside, and took a seat in the back row. She wondered how long she would be allowed to continue sitting there. Generally, Ruby's last-year's teacher warned her next-year's teacher about the impulsive and loud behavior of Ruby Northrop, and Ruby was instructed to sit in the front row of her new classroom, often directly opposite the teacher's desk.

Ruby watched her new teacher write *Welcome to Class 5A* on the blackboard while the rest of the students entered the room, some noisily, some quietly, all of them glancing at Mrs. Caldwell. The new teacher, who looked quite young, was wearing a sweatshirt with a large yellow daisy on the front. How horrible it would have been, Ruby thought, if *she* had worn her yellow daisy sweatshirt, too.

Ruby's mind wandered, and she was imagining herself onstage playing the role of Jane Banks in *Mary Poppins* when someone said, "Ruby?"

Ruby pulled herself away from the rooftops of old London and refocused her eyes. Before her stood Hilary Nelson. "We *are* in the same class!" cried Ruby. "Sweet! I knew we would be. Sit here next to me."

Hilary smiled but said, "I'm so nervous. You're the only person I know in this whole school."

"Well, that'll change soon," Ruby replied confidently.

"I'll introduce you to everybody. I have a very big mouth. I was the new kid last year, you know, and it really —"

"Attention, class!" Mrs. Caldwell called out. She closed the door to room 5A. "I think we're all here. Welcome to fifth grade. And Hilary Nelson, our new student, welcome to Camden Falls Elementary School."

The day began. Mrs. Caldwell introduced herself and took attendance.

Ruby was still seated next to Hilary in the back row.

Mrs. Caldwell handed out books and talked about what the class would be studying.

Ruby remained in the back row.

Finally, Mrs. Caldwell said, "Class, I want to tell you about one project we'll be working on that will last the entire year. I think you'll find it very interesting. How many of you remember hearing about the big hurricane that struck Florida last year?"

Ruby called out, "Hurricane Donna?"

"That's right," said Mrs. Caldwell, and Ruby braced herself for the reminder about speaking out of turn, but it didn't come. "Hurricane Donna," Mrs. Caldwell continued, "hit the east coast of Florida one year ago today. It destroyed several towns, and thousands of people were left without homes. A number of schools were destroyed, too, including the William Jefferson

Clinton Elementary School in Rawlings. Today the school will open for the first time since the storm. A friend of mine, Mrs. Samson, is a teacher at Clinton, and she told me that the school has been rebuilt but that it still needs books for the new library, and lots of equipment and supplies. Over the summer, I spoke with our principal, and Mrs. Samson spoke with the principal of Clinton, and we all decided that this year Camden Falls Elementary and Clinton Elementary will be sister schools. The students at our school will become pen pals with the students at Clinton, and we'll hold fundraisers to help Clinton purchase the books and supplies they need."

Ruby smiled. This sounded like fun. She couldn't wait to have her very own pen pal. "Will our pen pals be in fifth grade?" she asked.

"Yes," replied Mrs. Caldwell. "In fact, they're Mrs. Samson's students."

Mrs. Caldwell went on to announce that the first Clinton project would be a contest to design a symbol showing sisterhood between the two schools. "The winning symbol, or logo," Mrs. Caldwell continued, "will be silk-screened onto T-shirts that we'll sell to benefit Clinton. Logo entries are due next Wednesday, so if you want to enter the contest, you should start thinking about your design right away."

Mrs. Caldwell talked a bit more about Clinton and

the sister schools and various projects. When she stopped, Ruby looked at the clock. Nine fifty-two. Almost ten o'clock and she was still sitting in the back row.

That was a record for Ruby Northrop.

CHAPTER 6

Friday, September 5ᵗʰ

"You guys," said Flora on the first Friday of the new school year, a day that was warmer than the previous one, "I think we should sit at a different table at lunchtime."

Nikki, who had just stepped off her bus after another uneventful ride, removed her backpack and replied, "Okay. Can you believe how much homework we have already? This thing weighs a ton."

"I know," said Flora. "But we *are* in seventh grade now. That's what the principal was talking about at orientation — greater expectations and all."

Olivia thought, So *that's* what he was talking about. But what she said was, "Do we *have* to?"

"Do we have to what?" asked Nikki. She stooped down and picked up an acorn. "Look! This one's perfect.

I'm going to take it home and draw it." She dropped it in her pocket.

"Do we *have* to sit at another table?" said Olivia, a slight whine to her voice. She stopped walking, and Flora and Nikki turned around to face her.

"Don't you want to?" asked Flora.

"Not really. I like where we've been sitting."

"But I feel like we're hiding out." Flora glanced at Nikki.

"Me, too," said Nikki.

"You liked it on the first day. Both of you. You said so," muttered Olivia.

"Well, it *was* nice on the first day, when every single thing was new," said Flora. "But we can't hole up there all year long. We need to branch out."

Olivia didn't answer, and the girls walked into Central without another word. When they separated to go to their lockers, Flora whispered to Nikki, "You know we're going to sit somewhere else, right?"

"Yeah."

"What's Olivia going to do?"

"I'm pretty sure she'll come with us."

When fifth period began, Flora met Olivia and Nikki at the entrance to the cafeteria as she had done the previous two days. The girls joined the end of the line of students waiting to buy their lunches. Ten minutes later, their meals were paid for and they stood near the cashier, balancing their trays.

"Come on, you guys," said Olivia, eyeing their old table.

"No. Really, Olivia, we want to sit somewhere else," said Nikki.

"With other kids," Flora added as she scanned the room. "I see Tanya and Melody and Claudette. All at the same table."

"Who's that boy?" asked Nikki.

"I don't know, but let's go sit with them. There are plenty of empty seats at their table."

Olivia's stomach flip-flopped. "No," she said.

"Olivia . . ." Flora looked pleadingly at her friend.

"I don't want to."

"But we do. And we want you to come with us." Flora turned resolutely and threaded her way through the cafeteria until she reached the table. She now saw that three boys were sitting with Melody and the others, and she didn't know any of them. Still, she smiled brightly at Claudette and said, "Can we sit here?"

"Sure!" replied Claudette.

Olivia thought she heard Melody murmur, "It's a free country," but she was distracted by one of the boys who grinned at her and patted the empty chair next to him. Olivia gave him a tentative smile.

"Hey, everyone," said Claudette. "This is Flora, this is Olivia, and this is Nikki. They're from CFE, too. The boys," she went on, "are from Somerville. That's Max and David and Jacob."

Jacob was the boy sitting next to Olivia. Flora saw him grin again. "Olivia?" he said. "You're in my English class. With Mr. Barnes?"

"Oh," said Olivia. "Oh, yeah."

Claudette spoke up. "I have Mr. Barnes for English, too. He's cool. He said he just moved here."

Tanya made a face. "Who cares?"

"I —" Olivia started to say, then closed her mouth.

Melody yawned. "Can you believe all the homework we have already? What a pain. We're not supposed to have homework the first week of school."

Flora didn't see why not and was about to say so when Jacob announced, "Olivia's homework is always perfect." He looked at her admiringly.

Melody reached across the table and tweaked a French fry from Jacob's plate. "Really," she said flatly. "Huh." She waved the French fry in the air. "Do you mind?" she asked Jacob.

"Nope." Jacob's attention was on Olivia. "You're in my science class, too, you know," he said.

"*I'm* in your science class," said Melody, frowning. "With Miss Allen, hello?" But Jacob didn't hear her.

"How come you know so much about insects?" he asked. "Are your parents scientists or something?"

Flora suddenly felt like a proud parent. "Olivia's

♡ 36 ♡

practically a genius," she spoke up. "She skipped a grade."

"Hey!" exclaimed Jacob. "Me, too! What grade did you skip, Olivia?"

"Second."

"I spent second grade in France," said Melody.

"I skipped first grade," said Jacob.

"You did well on the science homework, too," said Olivia shyly.

Melody rolled her eyes. She reached for another French fry.

Jacob picked up his plate and placed it in front of Melody. "So you don't have to keep reaching," he said.

Flora saw a number of expressions cross Melody's face and realized Melody didn't know whether to feel surprised, grateful, or embarrassed. "Um, thanks," she said.

Flora glanced at Nikki, who had pursed her lips and was trying not to laugh.

"This could be interesting," Flora whispered to her, and turned her attention to her sandwich.

CHAPTER 7

Saturday, September 6ᵗʰ

"It's Saturday! It's Saturday!" cried Ruby the next morning. "They can make us go to school, but they can't take our Saturdays away."

In her room across the hall, Flora smiled to herself. "Who are 'they'?" she called.

Ruby waved her hand impatiently. "Whoever is in charge of these things. I don't care. Because today is Saturday and we're going to have another Saturday adventure, just like the Melendys."

Ruby lay on her floor. She was doing the yoga exercises she had invented for herself. Their purpose was to keep her brain and body in good working order, which was important for any performer. She was pretty sure that when she was doing yoga, she was supposed to clear her mind of extraneous thoughts, but Ruby was almost never able to do that. On this particular morning, her mind was on the summer's Saturday adventures.

Ruby remembered the day near the beginning of vacation when she and Min and Flora had arrived at Needle and Thread early in the morning and found the first four anonymous envelopes stacked by the door, one for her, one for Flora, one for Olivia, and one for Nikki. Inside each envelope the girls had found two books — *The Saturdays*, by Elizabeth Enright, and *Mrs. Frisby and the Rats of NIMH*, by Robert C. O'Brien — along with a letter from an unknown sender explaining that the girls were now members of a secret summer book club. Every few weeks they would receive a new book, and, like the Melendy family in *The Saturdays*, they would go on Saturday adventures.

Ruby was not an avid reader, and certainly not a fast nor even a very interested reader, but she had thoroughly enjoyed the books that had arrived in their anonymous packages all summer long, as well as the Saturday adventures the mysterious someone had arranged for her and her friends. She had especially enjoyed the last adventure, during which the identity of that mysterious person had at last been revealed. Madame X, as the girls had called her, turned out to be Ruby and Flora's very own aunt Allie, pretty much the last person Ruby would have expected. Allie, Ruby felt, didn't have much of a sense of humor and even less understanding of children. And yet she had done this spectacular thing for her nieces. As summer vacation had drawn to a close and the last adventure was ending, Ruby found herself wishing that their special Saturdays could go on and on. It was Nikki who had pointed out that they could — that the girls could think up adventures themselves. And so today they planned to set off on the first adventure of their own creation.

"Ruby? Are you done with your yoga yet?" called Flora.

Ruby jumped to her feet. "Done!"

"Come on, then. Min's in the kitchen making sandwiches for our picnic. Oh, I can't wait! This is going to be so much fun."

"Minnewaska, Minnewaska," Ruby chanted as she followed Flora down the stairs. "Have we been to Minnewaska before?"

"I don't think so," said Flora. "Not since we moved here, anyway."

Minnewaska, a state park located off the county road leading to Nikki's house, featured a clear lake in which Nikki said she had gone swimming many times, a large open area with picnic tables and barbecues, a playground, and hiking trails.

"Your mother and Allie used to love to go there when they were little," Min had told Ruby and Flora. "We'd have cookouts and picnics, and once your mother even held her birthday party there."

Ruby was impressed by this, but what she found

most exciting was the fact that Min, Nikki's mother, and Olivia's parents had agreed that the girls were old enough to ride their bicycles to Minnewaska without adults. It was to be a thoroughly independent day, and Ruby couldn't wait.

"Plus, our picnic is going to be really good," added Flora, "since Olivia's bringing the dessert."

Ruby closed her eyes rapturously. "I hope it's candy," she said.

The day was warm, warmer than Friday, and definitely warmer than Thursday, when the chill had been in the air. Good, thought Ruby, because I want to go swimming. The basket of Ruby's bicycle was packed with picnic food and a bag containing her beach towel and water shoes. As Ruby and Flora and Olivia pedaled along the county road, carefully riding in single file, Ruby sniffed at the air. She smelled wood smoke and damp earth and — was it possible? — sunshine. She hadn't realized until this moment that sunshine had its very own scent. The girls rounded a bend in the road then, and ahead Ruby saw an ash tree, its leaves already turning a translucent gold.

They rounded another bend, and there was a gate made from rough-hewn logs, and beyond it a sign bearing the words MINNEWASKA STATE PARK painted in yellow. Sitting under the sign was Nikki, her bicycle resting on its side. "Yay! You're here!" she exclaimed, and she hopped on her bike and led her friends along the road through the woods to the park.

"Oh, cool," said Ruby as the road came to an end. Before them spread the lake, the picnic tables, and the playground.

Nikki pointed to the woods that swept around the east end of the lake. "Over there are the hiking trails," she said.

"Wow," said Ruby. "What should we do first? Go to the playground?" She eyed a tall slide in the shape of a corkscrew.

Flora glanced at Olivia and Nikki. "Um, well . . . first let's chain our bikes to the rack and put our stuff on one of the picnic tables," she said diplomatically.

"And then the playground?" said Ruby. "Please?"

"How about a swim?" suggested Nikki. "While it's still hot."

"Yeah, we have to go swimming before we eat, anyway," said Olivia.

"All right." Ruby eyed the others suspiciously. She was about to strip off her T-shirt (she was wearing her bathing suit underneath) when she caught sight of two girls emerging from the lake, the sunshine gleaming on their dripping hair. "Hey, don't you know them?" she said, pointing. "They were in your class last year, weren't they?"

Flora looked toward the lake, then slapped Ruby's hand down. "Don't point!" she hissed, and at the same time Olivia said, with a small moan, "Oh, no. It's Tanya and Melody. Don't let them see us."

"Why not?" asked Ruby.

"Too late," whispered Nikki. "They're waving." Nikki waved back. "Hi!" she called.

"Are they coming over here?" asked Olivia. "I can't look. I really can't look." She concentrated on locking her bicycle to the rack.

"Nope," said Flora.

Ruby thought her sister sounded the teensiest bit disappointed. She frowned. "Well, do you all want them to come over here or not?"

"*SHH!*" hissed Nikki.

The girls locked their bikes, then carried their things to a table and spread them out. "Now where are they?" Olivia murmured to Ruby.

Ruby scowled at her as she said, "Sitting on towels by the lifeguard stand."

"Are they looking at us?"

"They're looking at the lifeguards."

"Figures," replied Olivia.

"Excuse me, can I just say something?" said Ruby. "No offense, but so far this isn't very much fun."

Nikki heaved a great sigh. "Well, let's go swimming, then."

Ruby smirked. "You're going to have to go right over there near . . . *them.*"

No one answered her.

For half an hour, the girls swam. Ruby paid close attention and noticed that Flora, Nikki, and Olivia managed to glance at Tanya and Melody approximately every three seconds.

When Ruby and her friends grew cold, they dried off. "I hope they don't think my bathing suit is too babyish," Olivia muttered.

The girls ate their lunch. Ruby was grateful that chocolate was involved but annoyed that the entire conversation centered around what Tanya and Melody would think of their food.

At last she said crossly, "I don't care what any of you say — I'm going to the playground."

"Don't hang upside down," Flora replied vaguely.

Half an hour later, Ruby was at the top of the slide, pretending to be Rapunzel and wishing she had longer hair, when she spotted Tanya and Melody crossing the park and climbing on their bicycles. The moment they were out of sight, Flora, Olivia, and Nikki ran to the playground.

"Cool slide!" exclaimed Flora.

Ruby, eight feet above the others, put her hands on her hips. "I don't understand you at all," she announced. But she tried to enjoy the rest of the Saturday adventure.

CHAPTER 8

Sunday, September 7ᵗʰ

Nikki and Mae sat on the front stoop of their weathered house. The afternoon was growing cool, and Mae hugged her knees to her chest. After a few minutes, she stretched out her legs and examined a bruise on her left knee. She had been unusually quiet on this long Sunday, a day on which Nikki had been in charge of Mae because their mother had unexpectedly been called in to work.

Nikki was about to ask her sister if anything was wrong, when Mae said, "We're like the take-away game."

"What do you mean?" asked Nikki.

"The take-away game. We play it in school. In math. Five take away one is four. Four take away one is three. Three take away one is two."

"Yeah?"

"Well, that's our family. First there were five people. Mommy and Daddy and you and me and Tobias. Then Daddy left. Five take away one is four. Then Tobias left. Four take away one is three. And today Mommy is gone."

"But she hasn't *left*," Nikki said quickly. "In fact, she should be home any minute. And Tobias is at college, but he isn't gone for good."

Nikki realized too late how that sounded. Sure enough, Mae said, "But Daddy *is* gone for good?"

Nikki looked across the yard at Paw-Paw, their beloved mutt, who was hunting field mice in the tall grass, rump in the air, forelegs on the ground as he sniffed and snuffled with great excitement. "Don't you want Daddy to be gone for good? Remember last Christmas?"

Mae said nothing.

"Mae?"

"I want *him* to be gone for good, but I still want a daddy. I didn't *really* want five take away one."

Nikki pursed her lips. She didn't know what to tell Mae about their father. So instead she said, "Well, look, we have Paw-Paw. Don't forget him. And Mommy's probably already on her way home. I bet if we go inside and start dinner, Mommy will walk through the door before you finish setting the table. Why don't you call Paw-Paw, and I'll see what's in the freezer."

In the Shermans' kitchen, Mae was carefully setting three places at the scarred wooden table when the phone rang. "I'll get it!" she shrieked, and she grabbed the receiver before Nikki could reach it. "Hello? . . . Hi, Mommy . . . She is here, but I want to talk to you. I can tell her the message . . . Okay . . . Okay . . ." And then, "But you *prom*ised. You promised you'd be home for dinner." Mae listened for a few more moments, then wordlessly handed the phone to Nikki.

"Aren't you going to say good-bye?" Nikki asked her.

"No."

Nikki spoke to her mother, then hung up the phone. "I think you hurt Mommy's feelings," Nikki said to her sister.

"Well, she hurt mine! She's not coming home for dinner."

"But when Mommy took this job, she told us that sometimes she would have to work on nights or weekends or even on holidays. It's a very big job. That's why she gets paid so well. Remember when she had *two* jobs and she hardly earned any money? This job is very important. She's in charge of the whole dining room at Three Oaks, where Flora's friend Mrs. Willet lives."

"I know," muttered Mae.

"I have an idea," said Nikki. "How about if we eat our dinner in front of the TV tonight instead of in the kitchen?"

"Okay. And can we have ice cream for dessert?" asked Mae piteously.

Tobias called that evening, and Mae grinned when she heard his voice on the other end of the line. "Nikki!" she cried. "It's Tobias! Get on the phone!"

Tobias told his sisters about his classes and that he had been to a football game the day before. At last he said, "Mae, do me a favor and go make me a drawing. Right now, okay? You can mail it to me tomorrow." When Mae hung up the extension, Tobias said, "So, Nikki — no word from Dad?"

"Nope. Nothing."

"Really?"

"Really. You know, Tobias, he doesn't know you got into college. He doesn't know you're not here."

"Mom might have told him."

Nikki hesitated. "I guess."

"So you have to stay on your toes. You have to be careful. Especially when you're there alone, but even when Mom is home."

"Okay."

Later, after Nikki had put Mae to bed, she sat in the kitchen, waiting to see headlights as her mother's car pulled into their lane. On the table before her was her history book, open to the beginning of Chapter Two. Nikki found herself reading and rereading the first paragraph without understanding a word of it. She heard Paw-Paw's nails clicking across the floor and jumped, upsetting a teacup. She jumped again when she heard a thump outside the front door. When she dared to peek through the window, she saw a startled raccoon blinking at her.

Nikki returned to the table. What if headlights swooped up the lane and her father's car appeared instead of her mother's? This might happen some evening. Her father could come back at any moment. After the previous Christmas, after a horrible scene that had taken place when her father *had* returned unexpectedly, Nikki had been convinced she would never see him again. Never. But nearly nine months had gone by since then — nine months in which her father might have changed his mind, nine months in which her mother might have written him, and in which Nikki herself had written him. She hadn't expected an answer to her letter (although she had wanted an explanation for a number of things), but who knew how Mr. Sherman's mind worked?

Nikki shivered and felt unreasonably relieved when at last her mother, looking tired but satisfied, stepped from her car and crossed the Shermans' yard.

CHAPTER 9

Monday, September 8th

Olivia liked all of her classes at Central. She liked her teachers. She even liked her homework. If she could simply go to school, learn, and come home, life would be wonderful. But school was so much more than learning. There were all the other students, for one thing, including, at Central, students who were as old as eighteen. Olivia had seen kids driving their own cars to school. She had seen kids who were a foot and a half taller than she was. She had seen girls who looked like ads for perfume commercials — endlessly more sophisticated than Olivia. Then there were the many extraneous aspects of school such as gym class and lunchtime and the trauma of lockers. Olivia imagined a cosmic vacuum sucking out of Central all the things that worried and annoyed her, leaving behind only the good things — learning and classes and teachers.

"Have you figured out your locker yet?" Flora asked as the girls passed the Fongs' art studio on their way to school Monday morning.

"Technically, no," replied Olivia.

"What does that mean?"

"It means I can use my locker, but the combination still doesn't work."

"How are you using your locker, then?" asked Flora.

Olivia glanced around as if someone on Main Street might be lurking, hoping to gain information about her locker. "I just *pretend* to use the lock," she whispered. "I take my stuff in and out, but the locker isn't actually locked. A locker that doesn't lock — is that an oxymoron?" she asked.

"I don't know. Olivia, aren't you afraid someone will break into your unlocked locker?"

"A little, I guess. But I don't keep much in it, and I always make sure to twist the dial around so it *looks* like the lock works."

"Huh," said Flora.

Olivia had a pleasant surprise when she entered Central that morning. Without thinking about it, and without consulting Nikki and Flora, she automatically made a left-hand turn, walked past the office, and began climbing the stairs to the second floor. She realized, as she led the way up the stairs and made another left, that she now knew her way to the junior high wing and could get there without thinking about what she was doing. On Friday morning, this route had seemed as unfamiliar to her as a road through a foreign country. Now she navigated it with assurance.

For this reason, when Ms. Garcia, her Spanish teacher, asked her that morning if she would take an envelope downstairs to the office, Olivia rose confidently to her feet, opened the door to her class, and strode into the hallway. She liked the halls of Central when they were nearly empty and she could saunter through them unimpeded. Central smelled exactly like Camden Falls Elementary, and if she closed her eyes, she could imagine that she was back in her old school on an errand for Mr. Donaldson. Olivia did close her eyes briefly but opened them when she heard footsteps. A student, definitely a high school student, was approaching her. She could be one of the perfume-ad girls, Olivia thought, and wondered what she was doing in the junior high wing.

The girl offered Olivia a puzzled smile. "Can I help you?" she asked.

"Um, no. No, thanks," said Olivia.

"You're not lost?"

"I'm just going to the office. I know the way."

"Oh, I'm so sorry." Olivia saw the flush that colored the girl's cheeks. "I didn't realize you were a student. I thought you were, well, never mind. Anyway, sorry."

It was Olivia's turn to flush. She knew exactly what

the girl had thought — that Olivia belonged in elementary school, that she was too small to be even a
seventh-grader at Central.

Olivia hurried on, head down, watching her feet.

She returned to her Spanish class just as Ms. Garcia
handed back Thursday night's homework assignment.
Ms. Garcia grinned as she dropped Olivia's paper on
her desk. The grin helped to lift Olivia's sagging spirits.
She looked at her paper. One hundred percent. Her
spirits rose a bit further. She glanced across the aisle at
Melody, whose paper had been dropped unceremoni-
ously on her desk, and saw Melody scowl. Olivia tried
to see the grade at the top of the paper, but Melody
covered it quickly with a bejeweled hand. She glared at
Olivia, and Olivia looked away.

Olivia survived another lunch at Melody's table,
mainly because she was separated from Melody by four
students. She talked to Nikki and Flora — and to
Jacob, who managed to sit next to her by pulling a chair
up to the table even though there was barely any
space.

It was a day of highs and lows, one after the other.
Olivia imagined them as the peaks and valleys on a
graph. If she could have taken hold of each end and
pulled, the peaks and valleys would become one
straight line, and that was her day — all the highs
diminished by the lows. Or were the lows diminished
by the highs?

Math class delivered one more high and low, and then another incident that Olivia had a bit of trouble classifying. High or low? She wasn't sure, but since she didn't want to end her day on a low, she decided to call it a high.

"All right, ladies and gentlemen," said Mr. Krauss. "Settle down, please. I have Friday's quizzes for you."

Olivia heard a loud and annoyed sigh and realized it had come from Melody, one row in front and two seats to the right of her. Olivia glanced at Mr. Krauss, but he didn't appear to have heard the sigh. He concentrated on walking up and down the aisles, dropping papers on desks. Olivia gazed with pleasure at the fat red 100% topping her quiz. The moment was spoiled, though, when she felt eyes on her and once again glanced up to discover that Melody was looking at her. Melody turned away quickly, though, poking the girl on her left (Olivia couldn't remember her name) and giggling.

"Ahem," said Mr. Krauss as he handed Melody her quiz. Melody faced forward, but Olivia could see that she was still smiling.

When all the papers had been returned, Mr. Krauss stood before his class, looking grave. "The results of the quizzes," he said, "have informed me that you could stand some review before we continue with the first chapter in our book." He tapped his head. "Your brain cells are still on vacation. We need to wake them up.

And so . . ." He reached for a stack of papers on his desk, and Melody let forth a groan. Mr. Krauss turned to her. "Miss Becker?" he said. "Do you have some sort of issue?"

Melody shook her head.

"May I continue, then?"

"Yes, go ahead."

Several students laughed but were silenced by the expression that crossed Mr. Krauss's face. "Miss Becker, please don't respond to what I'm about to say. I just want to inform you that you are treading on very thin ice." He reached again for the stack of papers. "These work sheets are a review of sixth-grade material," he said. "Not everyone in the class needs it, but it can't hurt anyone. The work sheets are to be completed right now, in class. And since this is a review, you may work with a partner if you like."

Mr. Krauss, with a number of severe glances in Melody's direction, passed out the papers. Several students switched seats so they could work in teams. Olivia put her head down and tackled the first problem.

She had finished four problems when she was aware that the boy beside her had left his desk and that someone else had slid into his seat. She felt a tap on her arm.

Melody was smiling sweetly at Olivia. "How come you're working alone? Mr. Krauss said we could work with partners. I pick you."

Olivia swallowed. "Me? I mean, you do? I mean, how come?"

"It's more fun this way." Melody swooped her hair over her shoulders with a great flourish. "You know, we're in a lot of the same classes, and I see you in the cafeteria. I even came to your party. But I feel like I don't know you. Here's my chance."

"Okay," said Olivia.

Melody considered the first problem on the sheet. "Huh," she said.

"What?" asked Olivia.

"Well . . ." Melody peered at Olivia's paper. "How did you solve this one?"

Olivia explained. And then she explained the second problem to Melody, and all the problems after that.

"Wow, thanks," said Melody when their sheets were completed. And she returned to her seat.

High or low?

High, Olivia decided.

CHAPTER 10

Tuesday, September 9th

So far, the September weather had been golden and clear, cool in the mornings and warmer by the afternoon. It made Flora think of pumpkins on the vine and frosty fields and piles of russet and red and dappled yellow leaves — even though it was too early for any of those things. But on Tuesday, the weather turned. Gone were the expanse of blue sky and the vibrant sunshine, and in their place were mist and fog and an unpleasantly wet breeze. Flora and Olivia walked down Main Street that gray morning, holding unopened umbrellas, the damp air curling Flora's hair into tendrils around her face and forcing Olivia's hair out of every one of its barrettes.

By the afternoon, Camden Falls's wet weather had settled in like an unwelcome guest.

"It's not supposed to break for at least a week," announced Min when Flora entered Needle and Thread after school.

"Oh, well," said Flora. "I kind of like it. It's cozy."

"What time is Mr. Willet going to pick you up?" asked Min.

Flora glanced at her watch. "In about ten minutes." She set her things behind the counter and looked around the store. No matter how often she entered Needle and Thread — even if she entered it ten times in a single day — she felt a rush of happiness at the sight of the bolts of fabric and racks of buttons, the projects and patterns and trims. Flora breathed in deeply, breathed in Needle and Thread's own particular smell, and called hello to Gigi and to old Mary Woolsey at work at her table near the back of the store.

"Min," she said, "I should take something to Mrs. Willet. Something I can talk about when I visit her this afternoon. What should I bring?"

"That's a tough one, honey. You know Mrs. Willet can't actually hold a conversation anymore, don't you?"

"Yes. But if I show her things, she looks at them. And I think she listens when I talk."

Min smiled at her granddaughter. "Why don't you take one of the sewing magazines with you? Mary

Lou used to enjoy sewing. Maybe you could read to her."

Flora had just selected the newest issue of *Creative Stitches* when she heard a car horn and saw Mr. Willet draw up to the curb outside the store.

"Bye!" Flora called to Min. "I'll see you later."

"Flora," said Mr. Willet, offering her a smile as she climbed into his car. "What a treat to have you along this afternoon. I really appreciate it. And so will Mary Lou. She loves having visitors."

Flora held up *Creative Stitches*. "I brought this so we can look at it together."

"That's a wonderful idea."

Mr. Willet drove carefully through the misty countryside. When Three Oaks came into view, he wound his way around the complex (Flora noted that the posted speed limit was 17 miles per hour) until he reached the visitors' parking lot. Moments later, he and Flora walked through the double doors and into the lobby.

"All right," said Mr. Willet. "We'll go downstairs and get Mary Lou. You can take her anywhere you like. She's especially fond of sitting here in the lobby and people watching. She also likes to sit over there" (Mr. Willet pointed to a couch facing out onto an expanse of lawn and gardens) "and look for rabbits and deer. My appointments today will take about an hour. So why don't we meet back here at quarter to five? Before we go home, I'll show you my apartment. It's empty, of course, but would you like to see where I'll be living?"

"Definitely," said Flora.

Flora enjoyed pushing Mrs. Willet's wheelchair through the hallways of Three Oaks. Three Oaks was quiet and peaceful, and Flora felt quite grown-up to have been entrusted with such a responsibility. She took care to walk slowly and carefully (she had once bumped the wheelchair into a wall as they turned a corner and Mrs. Willet's hands had flown to her mouth as she cried out) and to set the brakes on the wheelchair anytime they stopped to sit for a while. Sometimes Flora walked in silence, sometimes she narrated the world of Three Oaks for Mrs. Willet. "Look, there's Woody the parakeet. See his cage over there? And here's the gift shop. Min likes the gift shop. Oh, handmade baby sweaters. Wait, that's the window, Mrs. Willet. Don't knock on the glass." Flora wheeled the chair away from the shop. "Oh, there's a dog! Somebody brought her dog to visit! Maybe we can pat it."

They patted the dog. They watched people go in and out of the coffee shop. They peeked inside the beauty parlor. They sat by the windows and looked at the lawn. Every so often, Flora called out, "There's a rabbit, Mrs. Willet!" or "Oh, I see three deer. Do you see them?"

Mrs. Willet said, "Bumbumbumbum," and Flora didn't know what she saw.

By quarter to five, they had returned to the lobby and Flora was reading aloud from an article entitled "Bringing Heirloom Sewing to the 21st Century" in *Creative Stitches*. Mr. Willet, smiling, rounded the corner into the lobby.

"Darling!" Mrs. Willet suddenly exclaimed. "Is it really you?"

"It's really me," Mr. Willet replied, and kissed his wife's hand.

Mrs. Willet turned to Flora and whispered, "What's his name?"

Flora, embarrassed, said, "It's Bill."

"Bumbumbumbum."

Flora waited in the lobby while Mr. Willet wheeled his wife back to her room. When he returned, he said, "Ready for the grand tour?"

Mr. Willet led Flora through so many hallways and around so many corners that she felt as if she were back at Central on orientation day. She had no idea where she was.

"Here we go," said Mr. Willet presently. He stopped outside a door marked G-206, found a key in his pocket, opened the door, and stood aside so Flora could enter first.

"It's . . . it's lovely," she said, astonished at how depressing a completely empty space could look. All the walls were stark white and all the carpets were a pale yellow-brown that reminded Flora of cat litter.

"There are four rooms," said Mr. Willet proudly. "A bedroom, a guest bedroom, a living room, and a kitchen. And two bathrooms. The living room comes with a working fireplace. But this is the pièce de résistance." He ushered Flora to a set of glass doors at the end of the living room and slid them open. "A terrace. And I can have a garden here. I can put in anything I want. Maybe you and Ruby will come over next spring and help me plant it."

Flora swallowed. "Sure."

Mr. Willet looked very happy. And the expression on Mrs. Willet's face when her husband had returned had been one of pure joy, even if she couldn't quite remember who he was. The Willets belonged together; Flora knew that. But she couldn't imagine, simply couldn't fathom, leaving the Row Houses and moving into this bleak, blank space.

"Picture it with all my furniture inside," said Mr. Willet, as if he were reading Flora's mind.

And she tried very hard.

CHAPTER II

Wednesday, September 10ᵗʰ

"Let's not sit with Tanya and Melody today," said Nikki. She and Olivia stood against the front wall of the cafeteria, holding their trays and waiting for Flora to pay the cashier.

"Really?" exclaimed Olivia. "Really?! Wah-hoo! Let's go back to our old table."

"Well, I was thinking —"

"Okay," said Flora, joining them. "Sorry that took so long."

Olivia began threading her way between tables and chairs, stepping over backpacks and jackets, heading for the table that had been her island of safety the week before. "How come you don't want to sit with Tanya and Melody anymore?" she called over her shoulder.

"Olivia, come back here!" said Nikki. "I didn't mean —" She waited for Olivia to turn around.

Nikki and Flora watched as Olivia, tray teetering, returned to them. "What?" said Olivia.

"I was going to *say*," Nikki began impatiently, "that we thought we might sit over there."

She pointed to a nearby table — one of the quieter ones, Olivia noted. Already seated around it were Claudette, Mary Louise, Randall Tyler, and Sheldon Pecha, all from their sixth-grade class at Camden Falls Elementary. Olivia looked at the table at which Melody and Tanya were sitting. "I wonder why Claudette isn't with them," she said.

Nikki shrugged. "I don't know. But let's sit with Claudette and everyone, okay? Something different?"

"Even though they're from our old class?" asked Olivia.

"Yeah," said Flora. "Why not?"

Olivia followed Nikki and Flora across the cafeteria. "Can we sit here?" Nikki asked Claudette.

Claudette smiled at them. "Sure."

Olivia had just settled into her seat and stuck a straw in her juice box when Jacob appeared, flushed and somewhat out of breath. He dropped into the empty chair next to her.

"Hey!" cried a girl who had been about to sit in the chair herself and had nearly landed in Jacob's lap.

"Sorry," said Jacob, but he didn't move. "Hi, Olivia."

"Hi." Olivia looked across the cafeteria at Melody

and saw that she was glaring at Jacob, the seat across from her now empty. "Weren't you just sitting —" Olivia began to say.

Jacob waved a hand at her. "I wanted to sit with you, um, with you guys again." He arranged the items on his tray, all of which had slid to the right, and hung his jacket over the back of the chair.

On the other side of the table, Nikki grinned. "Jacob, do you know Mary Louise and Randall and Sheldon? They were in our class last year."

"Hey," said Jacob. He glanced at the pile of books by Olivia's tray. "How come you're carrying all those around?" he asked her.

Olivia flushed. "I don't, well, I . . ."

Jacob reached across Olivia and picked up the book on the top of the pile. "*Roll of Thunder, Hear My Cry*," he said. "What's that? Is it good?"

Olivia nodded. "I read it over the summer. We all did," she told him. "I mean, Flora and Nikki and I did."

"You all read the same book?"

"We had a book club," said Nikki. "It was really fun."

"At first it was a secret," added Flora.

"What do you mean, a secret?" asked Claudette.

Nikki and Flora and Olivia told the others about the secret summer book club.

"You guys are so lucky!" exclaimed Claudette.

"What else did you read?" asked Sheldon.

"*Mrs. Frisby and the Rats of NIMH*," said Nikki.

"*The Summer of the Swans*," said Flora.

"*The Saturdays* and *Understood Betsy*," said Olivia.

"We should have a book club," spoke up Jacob.

"Without the girl books," added Randall.

"What," said Jacob, "is the best book you've ever read? Everybody answer, starting with you, Olivia."

"*Roll of Thunder*," said Olivia instantly. "I'm reading it again right now. I think I'll read it at least once a year for the rest of my life."

Jacob turned to Nikki. "Oh, I can't choose just one," she said. "There are too many."

"Mine is *The Watsons Go to Birmingham*," said Mary Louise.

"When I was little," said Claudette, "my favorite book was *Wait Till the Moon Is Full*. Now it's *The Cat Ate My Gymsuit*. Or maybe *Bridge to Terabithia*. No, wait! It's *Tuck Everlasting*. Oh, I can't decide."

Everyone laughed.

"What's yours?" Olivia asked Jacob.

He scrunched up his face in serious thought. "*The Hobbit*," he said after a moment.

"Oh, I loved that!" cried Mary Louise.

"Hey, you know what, you guys. We really should start our own book club," exclaimed Nikki.

"With us? The eight of us?" asked Sheldon.

"And anybody else who wants to join. We could have it here at school."

"How do we start a club in school?" wondered Flora.

"Let's talk to Mr. Barnes," said Nikki.

"But he's new here," said Randall.

"He's a *teacher*," said Nikki. "Teachers always know how to do these things."

"You're going to start a book club?" said an incredulous voice. Nikki turned around to find Melody, hands on hips, addressing their table. "A *book* club? Oh, my God. That is so, like, dorky."

"Lots of people belong to book clubs," said Jacob evenly. He addressed Nikki again. "Okay. We'll talk to Mr. Barnes after school. We'll all go."

"*I'm* not going," said Melody.

"I didn't mean you," replied Jacob, and Melody stalked off.

"I know where Mr. Barnes's office is," said Nikki. "It's on the second floor near the main staircase." She looked at her watch. "Lunch is almost over," she added, "but this afternoon, we should all tell anyone we think might be interested in a book club to meet us at the office right after last period."

To Nikki's astonishment, nineteen seventh-graders crowded around the door to Mr. Barnes's office that afternoon. Nikki, Olivia, Flora, and Jacob explained what they wanted to do.

"We don't know *how* to do it, though," Nikki said.

"We don't even know how often we should meet or anything like that. We just know that a lot of kids are interested." She nodded toward the students waiting in the hallway.

"It's a terrific idea," Mr. Barnes replied. "So . . . I'll do a little digging and get some answers for you. Why don't we meet on Friday afternoon in my classroom and talk again then?"

Nikki turned to Flora and Olivia. "Yes!" she cried.

CHAPTER 12

Thursday, September 11th

Ruby stood on the corner of Main Street and Dodds Lane and considered Camden Falls on a dreary, wet September afternoon. She didn't ordinarily stop and pay attention to her surroundings (dreamy Flora was the one who did that), but Ruby had recently decided that if she was serious about becoming an actor, then perhaps she ought to be a more observant person.

"This is Main Street in Camden Falls, Massachusetts, on September eleventh," Ruby said to herself. She noticed that the shop windows seemed brighter than usual against the dull sky. She noticed that the streetlights had already come on, even though it was only mid afternoon. She noticed that the few trees that had begun to change color seemed almost to glow. She watched as a gust of wind sent a fistful of red and yellow leaves swirling around the door of Stuff 'n' Nonsense before they landed wetly on the pavement.

Ruby turned the corner and made her way up the block. She breathed in the smell of oregano and tomato sauce as she passed College Pizza. She stopped just long enough in Needle and Thread to call hello to Min and Gigi, to tell Min she was going to go to Hilary's apartment (eventually), and to stow her backpack behind the counter. Then she continued up the block, waving to Olivia's parents and Robby Edwards as she passed Sincerely Yours.

Ruby crossed the street, turned left, waved to Dr. Malone in his office and to Frank in Frank's Beans, studiously avoided horrible old Mrs. Grindle in Stuff 'n' Nonsense, and finally paused at the window of Cover to Cover to look at the display of children's books.

At last, she crossed Main Street again, then Dodds Lane, and stood before the Marquis Diner. The diner hadn't yet reopened, but the street in front of it was crowded with people and activity.

"Note the excitement, note the bustle," Ruby told herself.

"Ruby! Hi!" Hilary Nelson ran down the flight of stairs next to the entrance to the diner. "Come see what my new room looks like! When I left for school, the moving van was full and the apartment was empty. Now the moving van is almost empty and the apartment is almost full. Do you want to see?"

"Are you sure it's okay?" asked Ruby, eyeing the cartons on the pavement and the movers squeezing in and out of the doorway.

"It's fine," Hilary replied, and she took Ruby's hand and pulled her up the stairway. Halfway to the top, Ruby and Hilary had to stop and flatten themselves against the wall as one of the movers, sweating and out of breath, made his way back down the stairs, an empty carton in his right hand and four wooden dollies looped over his left wrist like enormous bracelets.

"Come on!" cried Hilary when he had lumbered by them, and she and Ruby ran to the top of the steps and through an open door. "This is it," announced Hilary. "Our new old apartment. It's very long. All the rooms are off this one hall. That's the living room in front. It looks out on Main Street, see? Then here's the kitchen. It has no window because it's in the middle. Here's the bathroom. Next is Mom and Dad's room." (Ruby noted that it had no window, either, and knew that Flora would feel claustrophobic in it.) "And back here where the hall stops are my room and Spencer's room. Can you believe we each have our own bedroom? They were one bigger room before the fire, but Mom and Dad decided to put up a wall to divide it in two. I know the rooms are small, but I like my privacy. And see, we each have a window."

Ruby looked out Hilary's window and said, "Hey, that's Aiken Avenue! You face my street." She peered around to the right. "You can't see our house, though. Oh, well."

Hilary plopped down on her bed. "Have you ever seen such a mess?" she asked.

Ruby nodded. "Yup. Last summer when Flora and I moved here. You should have seen our house. Practically every one of our neighbors came by to help. There were people everywhere."

"I forgot that you're new here, too," said Hilary.

"Well, not *new* new. Flora and I had visited Camden Falls lots of times when we were little. But then, you know, our parents . . . anyway, it was right after school ended last year that Min brought Flora and me back here to live." Ruby paused. "And on that first day my room looked pretty much like yours does right now."

"Ruby? Do you like living here?"

"Sure."

"But don't you miss your old life?"

"Do you miss yours?"

"Yes and no."

"I guess that's how I feel."

"Hilary?" called Mrs. Nelson from the other end of the apartment.

"I'm in my room!" Hilary turned to grin at Ruby. "*My* room," she said. "Not that stinky room in the rented house. *My own room.*"

Mrs. Nelson poked her head in the door. "Oh, Ruby, hello. I didn't know you were here."

"Hi, Mrs. Nelson."

"Hilary, I need you and Spencer to help me with the boxes in the living room, okay? Some of them belong back here."

"I'll help, too," said Ruby.

"Thanks." Hilary headed for the door.

"Wait," said Ruby. "Hilary, I have an idea. Can we open your window? Just for a second?"

Hilary raised her window and Ruby leaned out of it.

"Careful!" cried Hilary.

"I will be." Ruby craned her neck as far to the right as she could and then she exclaimed, "Hilary, I knew it! You *can* see my house from here! You can even see my exact bedroom window."

Hilary joined her new friend, and together they looked out over Aiken Avenue as lights came on in the Row Houses.

CHAPTER 13

Friday, September 12ᵗʰ

It was because Olivia had decided she needed money that she had to miss the Friday afternoon meeting in Mr. Barnes's classroom.

"Come with us. *Please?*" Nikki implored her at lunchtime. "You want to be in the book club, don't you?"

"Yes, but I begged Mom and Dad for a job in the store, and they didn't want to give me one at first. They said that Henry and Jack and I are kids, and just because our family owns a store doesn't mean we should be put to work in it. But I need money. Christmas is coming, after all."

"*Christmas?!*" Flora exclaimed.

"Yes. Christmas. Anyway, I made a big deal out of wanting a job, and finally — *finally* — Mom and Dad said yes. But they said I have to start small. Just one afternoon a week. And this is my first afternoon, so there's no way I'm going to miss it. You guys can tell me what happens at the meeting. Just don't suggest that the club meet on Fridays or I really won't be able to join it."

"All right," said Nikki.

And Flora added, "We know the job is important, Olivia."

When the last bell rang that day, Nikki and Flora made their way to Mr. Barnes's room, and Olivia headed for her locker. She stood in front of it and made a great show of twirling the dial around and around. Then she opened the door and removed the mountain of books she would need for her weekend homework. Several long-term projects had already been assigned, and Olivia wanted to get a head start on them.

Humming to herself, and still quite pleased with the fact that she felt confident navigating the halls of Central, Olivia hurried through the front doors and out into another moist, gray afternoon. Her hair had escaped the confines of her barrettes long before lunchtime, and now she didn't even bother to try to pat the stray wisps back in place.

By the time she reached Sincerely Yours, she was out of breath and vaguely damp — but excited about the prospect of her first day at work. She entered the store and deposited her books on the floor of her parents' office with a satisfying thump.

"Good heavens, Olivia! Did you bring home the entire library?" asked her father from behind the cash register.

Olivia smiled. "I have math homework, English homework, Spanish homework, and three projects to start. One of them is for science, and my teacher said I can do it on butterflies."

"Olivia! Hi! Good afternoon!" exclaimed Robby Edwards. Robby had begun working at Sincerely Yours over the summer, and recently the Walters, after a discussion with Robby and his parents, had increased his hours, a fact that pleased Robby immensely. "Are you ready to be an employee?" he asked Olivia.

"I'm all set."

"Do you know what your responsibilities are?"

"Well . . ." Olivia looked first at her father, who was now helping a customer, and then at her mother, who was overseeing the making of chocolates in the kitchen. "Actually, we didn't really discuss that."

"Do you want me to help you?" asked Robby.

"I guess." Olivia turned to her father. "Dad, can Robby tell me what to do?"

"Sure. But mostly we just need you to help customers with their baskets when the store gets busy."

At Sincerely Yours, customers could create gift baskets for any occasion, filling wicker baskets with soaps, trinkets, ornaments, small toys and books, and Mrs. Walter's homemade chocolates and baked goods.

"The important thing," said Robby, beginning to jump up and down, "is that the customer is always right. The customer is always right, Olivia! Do you know what that means?"

"Yes."

"Okay. And also, keep the shelves neat. But *I'm* in charge of making coffee. That's my job."

"Good," said Olivia, "because I don't know how to do that."

"I'm a champion," Robby announced. "Oh, look, here comes a customer. Do you want to help this one?"

"Okay," replied Olivia without turning around. "But only if he actually needs —"

"She. It's a *she*," said Robby.

And Olivia felt a tug on her sweater. "Hey!" cried a familiar voice. "I didn't know you would be here!"

"Oh. Melody," said Olivia. "I — I just started working here."

"Melody! Melody! I like that name!" announced Robby. "A name like a song."

Melody frowned, then turned away from Robby. "Olivia," she said, "I want to put together a basket for my mom's birthday. Can you help me?"

"*I* can help you," said Robby, his hands starting to flap. "I can help you, too."

"Oh, no, I don't think . . . I mean, well, Olivia's my friend and all."

I am? thought Olivia.

And Robby muttered, "Not nice, not nice," and edged away.

"Okay, here's the thing," said Melody, ignoring Robby. "I want to give my mom something really special for her birthday, but I don't have much money. I need expert advice."

"Well," said Olivia, "I'm pretty good at creating budget baskets."

"Excellent! What do I do first?"

"Start by choosing a basket. They're over here. Since you're on a budget, take one of the smaller ones."

"Really? A small one?" Melody wrinkled her nose. Then she whispered to Olivia, "Could you give me a break on a bigger one? A bigger one would look so much better."

"I guess . . ."

"Thanks. Now. What should we put in it?"

"The less expensive things are over here," said Olivia. "You can go a long way with soap and pens and little things like that. Because when you're all done, we'll wrap the basket in glitter cellophane and tie it with ribbons — for free. It'll look really cool."

"All right." With Olivia's help, Melody selected two bars of scented soap, a vial of bath salts, and a pen with a heart on the end.

"Perfect!" said Olivia. "Everything comes to about twelve dollars. That's not bad."

"But my mom would really like one of those picture frames," said Melody. "Oh, and that perfume."

Olivia shook her head. "Not for a budget basket."

Melody looked very sad. Then she said, "Olivia, I'd never ask this, except that we're becoming such good friends. I don't want to take advantage of you, but . . . you must get free stuff. I mean, it's your store."

"Not rea —"

"So maybe," Melody rushed on, "you could," she lowered her voice to a whisper, "just let me have those things for half price."

Olivia drew in a deep breath and was considering her answer when a loud voice from the next aisle said, "Olivia, that is not allowed." Robby peered at Olivia and Melody through a shelf of baskets.

"Excuse me," said Melody, "but I don't think this is any of your business."

"It's okay, Robby." Olivia led Melody to a corner of the store.

"What do you think?" asked Melody. "Half price? Please? I know you can do it."

Olivia knew she could not do it. But she said, "Well, since it's for your mother's birthday . . ."

"Thank you!" exclaimed Melody.

At the end of the day, after Melody had left the store in high spirits, and Robby, frowning at Olivia, had been picked up by his mother, the Walters gave Olivia her first afternoon's pay.

Olivia handed half of it back. "I let my . . . my friend Melody have some things for half price," she confessed.

"And you're paying the other half?" said her confused father.

"Don't ask," said Olivia. "It's not important. And it won't happen again. Really."

Olivia, looking at the pitiful amount of money left in her hand, wondered just what, exactly, she had done.

CHAPTER 14

Saturday, September 13ᵗʰ

The sign in the window of Needle and Thread read:

- HELP SUPPORT SHELTERING ARMS -
- MAKE A CAGE COMFORTER FOR
AN ANIMAL IN NEED -
- FREE SUPPLIES INSIDE -
- JOIN US TODAY -
- NOON TO 4:30 -
- EVERYONE WELCOME -

"Flora, this is so exciting," said Nikki. "Just think. Cage comforters for the cats and dogs at Sheltering Arms. Well, mostly for the cats. The dogs aren't in cages so much. But some of them are. And did you know that when an animal is adopted from the shelter, the cage comforter goes with him to his new home?"

Flora nodded vaguely. She and Nikki, Olivia, and Ruby were sitting squeezed together on one of the couches at the front of Needle and Thread. Approximately every thirty seconds, Flora pulled up her sleeve and looked at her watch.

"Flora! Quit checking the time!" exclaimed Ruby. "You're making me nervous."

"But it's almost twelve o'clock and no one's here yet."

"Maybe that's because it's *almost* twelve o'clock," said Ruby. "The sign doesn't say, 'Come in slightly before noon.' It says 'Noon.'"

Min called from behind the cash register, "For heaven's sake, Flora, you know people are going to show up. We've been advertising the workshop for weeks. Do you girls have everything set up in back?"

"Yes," said Olivia. "We're all ready."

The idea for the cage comforter project had been set in motion by Nikki, whose association with Sheltering Arms had begun the previous autumn. The Shermans' home in the country seemed to attract stray dogs, and softhearted Nikki had been only too willing to feed them — until so many were showing up each day that Nikki couldn't afford food for them all. Finally, Tobias had suggested that they talk to someone at the new animal shelter. Nikki, hesitant at first, had been pleased by her visit and with the help she had later received. When she learned that the people at Sheltering Arms tried to help the animals there feel more safe and relaxed by lining each cage with a colorful, padded "cage comforter," she had suggested to Flora that perhaps the next community sewing project for Needle and Thread might benefit Sheltering Arms.

"They always need cage comforters," she had told Flora. "And you know how many animals are there."

"I bet a cage comforter wouldn't be hard to make," Flora had replied.

And that had been the beginning. Min and Gigi had liked the idea, and this September Saturday had been selected as the date for the workshop.

"Well," said Flora now, looking at her watch for the umpteenth time (as Min would say), "it's noon exactly."

"And there's Mrs. Fong!" cried Olivia. "I'll bet she's here to help."

"Here comes Mr. Pennington, too," said Ruby.

By twelve-fifteen, every seat at the table at the back of the store was occupied. With the help of Min and Gigi, Flora and Nikki were explaining how to make a cage comforter.

"It's pretty simple," said Flora, "if you've done any sewing."

"And if you're not experienced," Gigi interjected, "we're here to help you."

"What you do," said Flora as she handed out sheets of instructions, "is choose two rectangles of fabric. We've already cut the fabric for you."

"In two sizes," added Nikki. "Smaller pieces are for the cages for cats and small dogs, larger ones are for the cages for big dogs."

"Then," Flora continued, "you cut out a rectangle the same size from this batting. The batting is padding for the comforters. You're going to sew the batting to the *wrong* side of one of your pieces of fabric —"

"The wrong side?" asked Mr. Morris, who had brought along Lacey and Mathias.

"Yup. You'll see why in a minute," said Nikki.

"You'll sew around all four sides," continued Flora, "then trim the batting close to the stitching. After that, sew the two pieces of fabric *right* sides together, and when you turn them inside out, the batting will be on the inside. Remember to leave an opening to turn."

"We'll show you how to finish the opening when you get to that point," added Min.

"So," said Flora, "the pre-cut fabric is there" (she pointed to the middle of the table) "and, well, I guess that's it."

"Ooh, ooh!" cried Lacey. "Look! I like this fabric." She reached for a piece of red fabric dotted with tiny cats wearing neckties. "Do you have to use the same fabric for both sides?" she asked Flora.

"Nope. Be creative."

This was followed by silence as the people around the table considered the fabric pieces — which Flora, Ruby, Olivia, and Nikki had spent hours cutting out.

Finally, Mr. Pennington said, "I'm going to make a small comforter and use cat fabric on one side and dog fabric on the other. That way, it could go in either a cat cage or a dog cage."

Mathias said, "I'm going to put stripes on one side and — oh, are these pigs? Pigs on the other side!"

"I want both sides the same," announced a little girl Flora didn't recognize.

Before long, sewing machines were humming and everyone was laughing and talking. Frank arrived with trays of coffee and tea and hot chocolate from Frank's Beans. College Pizza delivered sodas. Mrs. Walter sent Robby around with a tray of cookies from Sincerely Yours.

"I wish I could make one," said Robby, looking longingly at the growing pile of comforters in the middle of the table.

"Come back after your shift," said Olivia.

"Okay," said Robby. "And then I'm going to make *two*."

By four o'clock, Flora was exhausted. Stitchers had come and gone all afternoon. "Half an hour left," said Flora to Ruby. "I just counted the comforters. You know how many we have so far?"

"How many?"

"Forty-two."

"And you thought no one was going to show up," said Ruby. "Ha."

Two days later, Min drove Flora and Nikki to Sheltering Arms, the cage comforters carefully packed in bags. They carried the bags inside and presented them to Mrs. Hewitt, who had been helping Nikki with the stray dogs. Mrs. Hewitt beamed. And she invited Flora, Nikki, and Min to visit with the cats and dogs waiting to be adopted. Before Flora left that day, she watched as Mrs. Hewitt opened a cage containing a trembling cat, his tail tucked between his legs, and spread Mathias Morris's comforter on the bottom. The cat waited until Mrs. Hewitt had closed the door of the cage and stepped back. Then he stood, turned around twice, and settled himself on the comforter. Flora heard a small rumbly purr start up before she followed Mrs. Hewitt back to her office.

CHAPTER 15

Sunday, September 14th

Vincent Barnes, who handed out assignments to his students nearly every day, had given himself an assignment: By the end of September, all his boxes would be unpacked and his new house would be in order. He thought this sounded reasonable. It was mid September now, and he felt he was about halfway through the unpacking. The unpacking would have gone more quickly, he knew, if he had moved to Camden Falls over the summer, before school started, but he hadn't been able to do that. So the unpacking proceeded in its own time as the new school year unfolded — as homework was assigned and collected, as quizzes were graded, as teachers' meetings were attended, and now as the seventh-graders' book club took shape with Mr. Barnes at the helm.

Mr. Barnes's new house, which was actually a fairly old house, was cozy and charming and as different from the home in which he had grown up as anything he could imagine. There was a fireplace, which was large and constructed of fieldstone. There was a bay window looking out on East Elm Street. There were steps made of smooth unbroken stones leading to his front door. On the first floor were four rooms, including a dining room. On the second floor were three bedrooms. All this for one person. Also, there were one and a half bathrooms, and both toilets worked. So did all the kitchen appliances, the phone line, and the furnace.

Vincent Barnes stepped to the end of the couch he had placed in front of the bay window and reached for the curtain pull. He drew the curtains shut, then opened them again. In his boyhood house, his mother had kept the windows covered day and night, for reasons of safety. She said that if burglars couldn't see inside, then they wouldn't know whether anyone was at home. Burglar bars would have been more effective but were low on the list of things the Barnes family needed. Much higher on the list were running water, a working telephone line, a working furnace, and a working stove. All of these, except for the telephone line, were the landlord's responsibility, but he refused to return Mrs. Barnes's phone calls, and nobody in the family had the wherewithal to track him down.

The Barneses' rented house was so small it could

have fit handily inside the first floor of Vincent Barnes's new house. There was one bedroom, which Vincent and his brother and sister shared, while their mother slept on the couch in the living room — the only other room in the house apart from the bathroom and the useless kitchen. Above each window in the house was nailed a sheet or a portion of a sheet. These were never raised, and the interior of the house was dim all day long. Another sheet had been hung over a clothesline in the bedroom to separate the boys' side of the room from their sister's.

All these things Mr. Barnes saw clearly, even as he stood in his house — this house he owned — with its curtains and many rooms and working appliances. He saw, too, the high school to which he and the kids in his neighborhood had been bused. Most of those kids had been placed in remedial classes. But not Vincent. He had worked and studied and made his way into Advanced Placement classes, the only kid from his neighborhood to do such a thing. He hadn't spoken to the other students in the AP classes, though, and when school ended each day, he rode the bus back to his streets of boarded-up buildings and littered yards and went straight to the bedroom and worked and read until finally his brother would angrily and wordlessly turn out the light. If Vincent wasn't very, very careful with his books and assignments, they were apt to disappear from the bedroom.

When Vincent finally graduated from high school with a scholarship to a college in the Northeast, he said good-bye to his family and never returned to his old home. After he landed his first teaching position, he faithfully sent money to his mother every month until she died. He had no idea where either his brother or his sister was.

Now here he was in this first home that was all his own, finding a place for himself in a gentle and welcoming town. Every weekday morning he looked forward to arriving at Central High, and every afternoon he looked forward to returning to his house. On the weekends, he explored Main Street and took drives in the countryside. He had agreed to coach the seventh-grade boys' basketball team, and in addition, he would now oversee the meetings of the book club that some of his students wanted to start. He would let them choose all the books themselves, he decided. He would attend meetings only to monitor discussions and offer advice.

Mr. Barnes looked from the nine packing cartons in his living room to the sunny street outside. He opened the front door and breathed in the scents carried on the autumn wind. It was a humid day and the air was thick.

What, he wondered, would his students choose to read for their club? He considered handing them a list of some of his favorite books — *A Wrinkle in Time, Sounder, The Yearling, The Pigman, The Outsiders*, maybe

The Adventures of Tom Sawyer — but telling them that these were suggestions only; the actual choices would be theirs.

Around the corner of the house on his left ran two small boys and Max, a woolly dog of dubious lineage. "Hi!" the boys called to Mr. Barnes, and he waved to them.

A car drove down the street, followed by a truck and another car. Mr. Barnes sat on his stoop. He tipped his face to the sun. When he was young, he hadn't been allowed to sit on the stoop. Too dangerous, his mother had said, and she was right.

The front door of the house across the street opened and a woman hurried down the walk and climbed into her car. She had introduced herself to Mr. Barnes on the day he had moved in. She had said that she, too, was new to the neighborhood. Her name was Allie Read and she was a writer. Mr. Barnes had been impressed. He had read some of her books. He wondered now if she was working on anything new.

Mr. Barnes checked his watch and stood up. Better unpack a few more boxes. Maybe, he thought, recalling the sight of Max romping through the yard, he would get a dog.

CHAPTER 16

Monday, September 15th

Ruby hustled through the halls of Camden Falls Elementary, Hilary Nelson in front of her, awful Andy Cheney behind her. Andy liked to step on the backs of people's heels, so Ruby hopped from side to side, avoiding him, as her class made their way to the auditorium.

"Isn't this exciting?" Ruby said to Hilary, sidestepping Andy once again. "I can't wait to see who won the contest."

Ruby felt that this was going to be a good day. She had felt it from the moment she woke up, because when she opened her eyes, she had found King Comma staring at her from the foot of the bed. A staring cat, Ruby thought, was a good sign. Sure enough, the first thing Mrs. Caldwell had said to her students that morning after she had taken attendance and collected homework was, "Class, I have a surprise for you. At today's assembly, the winner of the T-shirt design contest will be announced. And," she went on as Andy let out a whoop followed by a belch, which she ignored, "the announcement will be made by a special guest."

"Mayor Howie?" asked Ruby, who had met Camden Falls's mayor on more than one occasion.

Mrs. Caldwell smiled and shook her head.

"Somebody's mom?" asked Ava Longyear.

"Nope. Our special guest is . . . Mrs. Samson," said Mrs. Caldwell. "She's traveled all the way from Florida to talk to our school today and to tell us more about Clinton Elementary. And this afternoon, she's going to visit our classroom to tell us about her students. They're going to become your pen pals, so Mrs. Samson will give each of you a letter from your pen pal, which you can answer, and she'll hand out your letters to her students when she returns to Florida. After that, you'll correspond with your pen pals by mail."

Ah–ha, thought Ruby. So I was right. A staring cat *is* a good sign.

Now Ruby and her classmates were on their way to the assembly, Ruby nimbly avoiding the tips of Andy Cheney's shoes.

"I wonder how many kids entered the contest," said Hilary, turning around to glare at Andy, since Ruby was now accidentally stepping on Hilary's heels.

"Eighty-one," Ruby replied instantly. "I heard Mrs. Caldwell say so on Friday."

"Wow. Eighty-one. That's a lot."

"You worked really hard on your design," said Ruby, who had spent very little time on her own design.

"I thought about it while we were packing up to move."

Hilary's finished design showed an outline of the eastern coastline of the United States, Florida on the bottom, Maine on the top. Standing over Florida was a boy who extended his hand to a girl standing over Massachusetts. Their hands met in the middle, each holding one edge of an open book. "See?" Hilary had said to Ruby on the day they handed in their designs. "The kids in Massachusetts and Florida are reaching out to each other and learning from each other. That's what the book represents — learning, and also the books we'll be buying for the new school."

Ruby had been impressed. Her own design had shown an open book, too, on the left page of which she had written *Massachusetts* and on the right page of which she had written *Florida*.

"What does it mean?" Flora had asked when Ruby had shown her the design.

"I don't know. It's just, you know . . . books and states . . . and . . . I guess that's it."

Ruby and her classmates now settled into their row of seats in the auditorium. Presently, their principal, Mrs. Covey, walked onto the stage. She greeted the students and talked to them about Hurricane Donna and the destruction it had caused in Rawlings, Florida, and the surrounding towns. "And," she said, "here to tell you more is Juliette Samson, a fifth-grade teacher at Clinton Elementary and a friend of Mrs. Caldwell, one of our own fifth-grade teachers."

Mrs. Samson, a cheerful-looking woman wearing a Clinton Elementary School T-shirt, crossed the stage, shook Mrs. Covey's hand, took the microphone, and said, "Thank you, students and teachers at Camden Falls Elementary. I want to tell you how grateful everyone at my school is that you've agreed to help us. Clinton wasn't the only school destroyed by the storm. Lots of schools need help, so we're doubly thankful for yours. I'd like to begin by showing you some photos of Rawlings before and after Hurricane Donna."

"Goody," Ruby whispered to Hilary as the lights in the auditorium dimmed. "A slide show."

Ruby felt her glee fade, though, as she watched images of sunny streets and smiling faces and trim stucco homes become images of piles of rubble and houses that had been ripped from their foundations. There was even a photo of a mud-spattered dog, clearly lost, trailing his battered leash behind him.

"This," said Mrs. Samson eventually, "is Clinton Elementary before the storm." Ruby looked at a photo of a school not unlike Camden Falls Elementary, except that it was situated in a grove of palm trees. "And here's our school after the storm."

Ruby gasped. So did Hilary and most of the students in the room. Ruby could tell that the second photo had been taken from the same spot as the first. But she couldn't find an actual building in the picture — merely a pile of crumbling stucco, a number of fallen trees, and a large amount of wet trash.

"But," Mrs. Samson continued, "this is what our school looks like today." A third photo was flashed on the screen above the stage, and now Ruby saw a brand-new building. "It's beautiful, isn't it?" said Mrs. Samson. "But, as I'm sure your teachers have explained to you, our library is still nearly empty, we have only a few textbooks, and we need computers, sports equipment, and all sorts of supplies. Those are the things you'll be helping us with this year. And for which we're very, very grateful."

Everyone applauded, and Ruby joined in, but her mind was on the images of the dog minus his owner and of Clinton Elementary after the storm. For a moment, she felt tears prick her eyes, and she bit her lip. She was absolutely not going to cry here. Not with Andy Cheney sitting next to her.

Later, Ruby applauded loudly when Mrs. Samson announced that the winner of the contest was Hilary, and she turned to hug her friend before Hilary made her way to the stage to accept the very first T-shirt with her own design on it. Ruby's glee had vanished, however. Contests and assemblies and bake sales and new books were fine, but now Ruby knew what lay behind them.

That afternoon when Mrs. Samson handed her a letter from her pen pal, Maya Sanchez — a very nice letter describing Maya's family and her first day in her rebuilt school — Ruby, who that morning had mentally been composing a letter about her new tap shoes and about how much allowance money she had saved up, instead wrote the following note to Maya:

Dear Maya,

Hi, my name is Ruby Northrop and I'm your pen pal. Thank you for your letter. I really liked hearing from you. I am very, very, very, very, very sorry about Hurricane Donna and what the storm did to your home and your town and your school. I can't imagine losing any of those things. We are going to work hard here in Camden Falls to help you buy books and supplies for your new school. What do you need the most of all?

Your new friend,
Ruby Northrop

P.S. I'm glad your cat survived the storm. I have a cat, too. His name is King Comma. Yesterday he ate a moth.

CHAPTER 17

Tuesday, September 16th

Olivia's complicated schedule at Central allowed her —
at least during the first quarter of the year — two
study periods each week, one on Tuesday and one on
Thursday. Olivia both appreciated them and dreaded
them. She appreciated them because they allowed her
to get a jump on her homework. She dreaded them
because Flora and Nikki had art class at this time, and
there was not a single student in the rest of the room
that Olivia knew well. The other students were in
grades seven through nine, and while most of them
paid not a bit of attention to her, Olivia still felt little and awkward, sitting alone hunched over her papers
and textbooks while around her kids talked and
laughed and ran from desk to desk seeking homework
help from their friends.

On Tuesday, Olivia was deeply involved in an extra-credit math problem (math came easily to her and she enjoyed a good challenge) when she was startled by a perfumed body sliding into the chair next to her.

"Hi!" chirped a very perky voice.

"Melody!" exclaimed Olivia. "I didn't know you had study period now."

Melody waved her hand around, indicating the large number of students in the room. "There are so many kids here. I've been sitting all the way over there." She pointed across the room. "So," she said, "how are things going?"

"Fine," Olivia replied cautiously. She thought the question odd, since she had already spoken to Melody several times that day.

"Good. How's the store?"

"Sincerely Yours? Um, it's fine. Too."

"It's such a great place. My mom really liked her birthday basket."

"Oh, I'm glad," said Olivia, feeling a pang as she remembered the skeptical looks on her parents' faces as she handed back half her pay.

Melody opened her science book. She opened her notebook. Olivia realized she was settling in to work.

"Did you do our science assignment yet?" asked Melody.

Olivia's mind was still half in the math problem.

"The science assignment?" she repeated vaguely. "Which one?"

"The one that's due tomorrow."

"Yes." Olivia froze. She abandoned thoughts of numbers. Her mind was now entirely on Melody.

"Can I see it?"

Olivia released an inward sigh of relief. "I already handed it in to Miss Allen."

"You already handed in tomorrow's assignment." Melody said this flatly, a statement not a question. She tilted her chin and raised an eyebrow.

Olivia nodded. "I did!" Why did she feel as though she needed to explain herself?

"What for?"

"Excuse me?"

"Why did you hand it in early?"

Olivia shrugged. "Because it was done."

"Oh, well," said Melody. "I guess that's all right. If it's done, that means you know all the answers." She pushed her science book toward Olivia, shoving Olivia's math book out of the way in the same motion. Then she leaned over, chin in hand, and, wielding a pen, indicated the list of questions that were to be answered. "I'm having trouble with these," she said.

Olivia sighed and closed her math book. She would have to finish the problem at home. "The answers to these questions are in Chapter Two —" she started to say.

"I know *that*," snapped Melody.

Olivia sighed again. "All right. Let me show you how to figure them out."

Melody snorted. "You don't understand. I don't want help with them. I want you to do them."

"*For* you?" squealed Olivia.

"Yes, *for* me."

"But I can't. That would be cheating."

Melody snorted again, and Olivia saw that she was looking across the room at her friends. And the friends were watching Olivia and Melody.

Olivia tore her gaze away from them and focused on Melody. "Look, I don't *have* to do the problems." She was going to add "And you can't make me" but changed her mind.

"No. I guess not," replied Melody. "It's just that the other kids thought it would be nice if you helped me out, since you're so smart and all. They don't know you very well. They think you're kind of . . . anyway, you want friends here at Central, don't you?"

Olivia felt like a mind reader, understanding that what Melody meant to say was, "You don't want enemies here at Central, do you?"

"Well," said Olivia in a small voice, "okay." She peered at the first question. "The answer to this one is . . . do you want me to write them out for you, too? Don't you think you should hand in the assignment in your own handwriting?"

"Whatever." Melody poised her hand over her note-book. "Go ahead. Dictate."

And Olivia did.

"Is that really what she said?" asked Nikki incredu-lously. "'Go ahead and dictate'?"

"Pretty much," Olivia replied miserably. She and Nikki and Flora had gathered at Needle and Thread that afternoon.

"And so you did?" said Flora.

Olivia nodded.

"But why?" asked Nikki.

"Because all her friends were watching, and Melody implied that if I didn't help her out, I'd make enemies at school."

The girls were silent for a moment.

"How much power do you think Melody has?" won-dered Flora.

"She's not a wizard," said Nikki, who sounded more vehement than she felt.

"Well, anyway, you can't tell a *soul* what I did," said Olivia in a loud whisper. "Seriously. My parents would kill me. And Miss Allen would accuse me of cheating."

"Excuse me, but isn't Melody the cheater?" asked Flora.

"If I do her work for her, then I'm just as much a cheater," said Olivia. "It isn't like she copied my work and I didn't know about it. So not a word to anyone. Swear. You have to *swear*." Olivia's voice wobbled.

"Okay, okay. We swear," said Nikki, glancing at Flora.

"Yeah, we swear. We won't tell anyone."

"Not even Ruby," said Olivia.

"Not even Ruby?" Flora sighed. "That's going to be really hard."

"Well, maybe we'll tell her later. But right now — pinkie swear you won't tell *any*one."

"We already said we swear," said Nikki.

Olivia nodded. "Okay."

CHAPTER 18

Wednesday, September 17ᵗʰ

The gray weather that had descended on Camden Falls the previous week had lifted on Tuesday, only to return the next morning.

"It figures," said Flora sullenly to herself as she and Nikki and Olivia walked to Main Street after school. She scuffed her feet through falling maple leaves.

"You know what I like about gray days?" asked Nikki cheerfully.

"What?" said Olivia.

"They make all the colors look brighter than usual. Especially the colors of the leaves."

"Definitely," replied Olivia.

Flora said nothing. She stared at the sidewalk.

Nikki poked her. "Something the matter?"

"Yes."

"Well, are you going to tell us what it is?"

"I guess. You'll find out sooner or later, anyway. Let's go to Frank's Beans and get something to drink. I'll tell you there."

Frank's was featuring a fall drink called Pumpkin Spice Chai, and Flora and her friends each ordered one, then found an empty table at the back of the store.

Olivia sipped her drink. "Huh," she said. "It's . . . huh . . ."

Nikki tried hers. "Pumpkin-y."

Flora looked blankly at hers. She swirled her straw through it. At last, she said, "Tonight Min and Mr. Pennington are going on a date."

Olivia let out a yelp and Nikki spit a mouthful of chai across the table.

"What?" cried Olivia. "Seriously?"

Flora nodded. "Seriously. Min told Ruby and me at breakfast this morning."

"They do spend a lot of time together," said Olivia slowly. "Min and Mr. Pennington, I mean. They go out to dinner and stuff."

"But I never thought they were *dating*," said Flora.

"I didn't know old people *could* date," said Nikki, wiping the table with a napkin. She tossed the napkin in a trash can. "How old *is* Min, anyway?"

"Seventy-two," Flora replied.

"And how old is Mr. Pennington?"

"I don't know. Like eighty or something."

"Why are they going out on a date on Wednesday night?" asked Olivia. "Why not on Friday or Saturday?"

"Could we focus here?" said Flora. "That is not the issue."

"If you're going to be touchy," said Olivia, "then I'm not going to discuss this with you."

"Sorry," muttered Flora.

"You know, this is surprising news," said Nikki, "but it's a good thing. Isn't it? Why are you so upset, Flora? You love Min. You love Mr. Pennington. Why don't you want them to go on a date?"

"I don't know. I just don't." Flora stared at her chai. "I don't think I want this after all."

Min left Needle and Thread earlier than usual that afternoon, and Flora and Ruby walked back to Aiken Avenue with her, Ruby peppering her with questions.

"Where do you think you're going to go tonight?"

"Fig Tree, most likely," Min answered. "That's sort of our special place."

"You already have a special place?" exclaimed Ruby. "Cool. What are you going to wear?"

"Why don't you help me choose something?" said Min.

Daisy Dear gave Flora, Ruby, and Min a joyous and very wiggly greeting when they opened the door of the Row House. Flora took her on a walk up and down Aiken Avenue, and by the time she returned, Min was wearing the emerald-green dress Ruby had chosen for her and was standing at her bureau, considering her jewelry.

Flora stood in the doorway, one hand on her hip. "When," she said, "did your dinners with Mr. Pennington turn into dates?"

Min eyed her in the mirror. "I don't have an exact timetable for you, Flora." She paused, started to say something else, then closed her mouth.

Flora looked at Ruby, who was lying on her stomach on Min's bed, watching the getting-ready-for-a-date process. And she remembered when she was younger than Ruby and had liked to sit in the armchair in her parents' bedroom in order to watch her mother get ready to go out with her father. Her mother had had a dressing table with a white skirt around it and a blue stool that slid under the table and hid behind the skirt. She would pull the stool out and sit on it while she applied her makeup and poked through her jewelry box. At last, she would scrutinize herself in the mirror (the one with photos of Flora and Ruby stuck under the edges of the frame) and she would spin around on the stool until she was facing Flora and say, "What do you think?"

And Flora would reply, "What about perfume?"

And her mother would say, "You choose."

Flora would leave the chair and stand beside her mother, looking over the row of glass bottles. She always chose the same perfume. She didn't know what it was, but it came in a bottle the exact color of the roses on the bush by their front door.

Flora's mother would put one drop behind each ear and then Flora would pronounce her "Perfect."

Flora now looked at Min, who had selected a pair of earrings that Flora thought looked cheap and also too big. She turned away and retreated into her bedroom.

"Flora's jealous!" she heard Ruby call.

"I am not!" Flora shouted. But she thought Ruby might be right. She just didn't know whom she was jealous of — Min or Mr. Pennington.

Or why.

Shortly before Mr. Pennington arrived to pick up Min, Aunt Allie walked through the front door. "How are my favorite nieces?" she asked.

Ruby giggled. "We're your *only* nieces."

"Well, you're still my favorites. And I'm glad I get to spend the evening with you. How are you, Flora?"

"Fine." When Flora heard the doorbell ring a few minutes later, she stomped up to her room and stayed there until she heard the front door close and the sound of a car starting on the street below her window. When she went downstairs again, Aunt Allie was on the phone with College Pizza.

"We get to order pizza for dinner!" announced Ruby. "Min said so. You missed hearing her because you were sulking in your room."

"Uh-huh," replied Flora.

"So," said Aunt Allie after she hung up the phone, "tell me what's going on. Tell me everything."

Ruby launched into a detailed account of Clinton Elementary and Maya Sanchez and the T-shirts that were being made up with Hilary's design on them.

"My goodness," said Aunt Allie. "That's a lot of information. What about you, Flora?"

"Flora's mad because Min's on a date," said Ruby.

"Ruby," said Aunt Allie.

"Sorry."

"I am not mad," said Flora, and she tried to think of something cheerful to tell Aunt Allie, just to prove how not mad she was. "Guess what," she said after a moment. "The kids at school liked the idea of our summer book club so much that we're starting a book club at Central. A lot of kids want to belong to it. Isn't that great? And it's all because of you."

"Why, Flora. I'm — I'm honored," said Aunt Allie. "Truly. That means a lot to me."

Flora could feel her good humor start to return. She ate pizza with Ruby and her aunt. She tackled her homework. She phoned Nikki. When Aunt Allie asked if she and Ruby wanted to have an overnight at her house on Friday, she said yes. And when Min walked through the door just before nine-thirty, she apologized for her earlier behavior and told Min she loved her.

CHAPTER 19

Thursday, September 18th

Ruby could remember in great detail the dramatic fire that had destroyed the Marquis Diner at the beginning of the summer. She remembered being jerked from sleep in the middle of the night by the sound of sirens and the smell of smoke, remembered peering out her bedroom window and watching fire engines shriek around corners and turn onto Main Street. Ruby didn't know Hilary or any of the Nelsons then. Neither did most people living in Camden Falls. But by the end of the summer, nearly everyone knew them and in some large or small way had helped them rebuild the diner.

Now it was September (just three months since the fire, thought Ruby with wonder), the diner had been rebuilt, and this evening the Nelsons planned to hold the grand re-opening. Ruby, dressed and ready to go, kneeled on her bed and looked out her window across

Aiken Avenue toward Main Street. By now she could easily find the window of Hilary's bedroom, although she did have to strain to see it. In winter, when the trees were bare, the view would be better.

"Ruby? Are you ready?" called Flora from downstairs. "Min and I are waiting for you."

"Coming!" called Ruby. She clattered down the steps, saying, "Oh, this is going to be so exciting. A party! Everyone will be there. And tomorrow the diner will be back in business. Hilary said there are going to be door prizes tonight." She paused. "What are door prizes? Oh, well. I guess we'll find out. Not actual doors, I hope. That would be weird. And everyone who comes is going to get a coupon for a free sandwich. . . . Come *on*, you guys! Hurry up. We don't want to be late." Ruby hurried out the door ahead of Flora and Min, whom she left smiling in the hallway.

"Whoa. Look," said Ruby a few minutes later as she rounded the corner onto Main Street. "Look how many people are here."

The window of the Marquis Diner was swathed in red-white-and-blue bunting, beneath which was a sign announcing the grand re-opening. Ruby, peering through the doorway, could see a large crowd and hear the sound of laughter and a great many people all talking at once. "There's Hilary! I see Hilary!" Ruby called over her shoulder to Min and Flora. "Oh, and there's

Robby and his parents, and Sharon from the pet store, and Mr. Samuels from the grocery store, and Frank and — hey, is that Frank's wife? I bet that lady is his wife."

"Ruby, you need to calm down a bit," said Min quietly, taking Ruby by the elbow.

"Okay. Hey, hi, Hilary! Hi!"

"Hi, Ruby," replied Hilary, pulling her friend inside. Hilary was carrying a basket, and she removed three slips of paper from it and handed one each to Ruby, Flora, and Min. "These are your sandwich coupons," she said. "Good for six months."

"And these are for the door prizes." Spencer stepped around his big sister and pulled three red tickets from a large roll.

"What *are* door prizes?" asked Ruby suspiciously. "I already have a door."

"They're really cool," said Spencer. "One lucky winner will get an iPod and one will get dinner for four at the diner."

"An iPod! *I* want an iPod!" cried Ruby.

"Well, tear off the ticket stub and don't lose it," said Hilary. "Drop the rest of the ticket in the soup pot over there. And keep your fingers crossed."

Ruby carefully tore her ticket in two and put the stub in her pocket. Then she made her way through the crowd to a large ceramic pot bearing a sign that read DRAWING AT 8:00. She dropped her ticket in the pot and stepped back to look around the room. She had just spotted Lacey Morris sampling teeny sandwiches with Alyssa and was about to call to her, when she heard someone laugh and say, "I've got her doing half my homework for me."

The laugh was nasty, and Ruby stopped and turned around. A familiar-looking girl was standing with two other girls under a large photo of Judy Garland.

"What? Who's doing your homework for you?" asked one of the others.

"Her." The first girl pointed across the diner. "You know. Olivia Walter. The smart one."

Ruby gasped. The girl was one of the two who had been at Minnewaska State Park. When Ruby looked in the direction in which she was pointing, there was Olivia, all right. She was talking with Flora and Robby. Ruby turned back to the group of girls. They were laughing. She narrowed her eyes at them.

One of them noticed her. "Something wrong?" she asked.

"No," said Ruby. "No." She pushed her way through knots of people until she reached Olivia. "Excuse me, you guys," she said to Flora and Robby. "I have to talk to Olivia. In private." She hauled Olivia to a quiet corner and told her what she had overheard. "Is that true? What did she mean when she says she *has* you doing her homework for her? That doesn't sound very nice. It sounds —"

Olivia clapped her hand over Ruby's mouth. "*Shh!* I don't want anyone to know about this." She glanced around the diner.

"But, Olivia —"

Ruby struggled, but Olivia's hand remained clamped firmly in place. "I said, *shhhh!*" said Olivia.

"Take your hand off," Ruby tried to say.

"Not until you promise to keep this a secret."

Ruby stuck out her tongue and licked Olivia's fingers.

"Oh, ew!" squealed Olivia. She jerked her hand away and wiped it on her jeans. "Ruby, seriously, you can't tell anyone. Only Flora and Nikki know about this."

"You told Flora and Nikki and you didn't tell me?" Ruby's voice was rising.

"I was going to tell you, but I hadn't seen you."

"Really? You were going to tell me?"

"Um, yes."

"So tell me now."

Olivia led Ruby outside the diner and hurriedly whispered the story to her.

"Man," said Ruby. She peered through the window. "Where are those girls? Where's Melody? I'm going to —"

"Ruby," said Olivia sternly. "I mean it. Keep quiet. I'll figure this out."

"Okay." Ruby tried to enjoy the rest of the party. She sampled a vegetable kabob. She helped Hilary hand out the coupons. She shared an ice cream sundae with Alyssa. And she listened with interest when the door prizes were announced. (She didn't know the winners.) But she couldn't stop thinking about Melody and Olivia and the homework assignments and the fact that someone was bullying one of her best friends.

From across the diner, Ruby Northrop gave Melody Becker the evil eye.

CHAPTER 20

Friday, September 19ᵗʰ

Surprises, Flora thought, happened when you least expected them. Well, of course they did. That made sense. If you expected them, they wouldn't be surprises.

Flora had a very surprising Friday. One of the most surprising things was that after a fairly routine day, Flora experienced one surprise after another that night, until finally she was surprised by the sheer number of surprises. Who would have thought she'd have so many surprises in just one evening?

"Ready, girls?" asked Min the moment she returned from Needle and Thread.

Flora and Ruby, who had been on their own in the Row House that afternoon, chorused, "Ready!"

"We packed all our stuff in one bag," announced Ruby. "One bag for both of us."

"Did you remember your toothbrushes?" asked Min. "Your nightgowns? Clothes for tomorrow?"

"Yes, yes, and yes," replied Flora.

"We're only going to be at Aunt Allie's," Ruby pointed out as she and Flora followed Min to the car. Then she added, "Min? Do you think you'll be lonely tonight?"

"I'll have Daisy Dear and King Comma for company," Min replied. She didn't point out that until her granddaughters had come to live with her, she had spent every night alone.

Min drove slowly through the streets of Camden Falls, Daisy sitting solemnly beside her, eyes focused straight ahead, on the lookout for squirrels.

As Min pulled into Allie's driveway, Flora suddenly exclaimed, "Hey! There's Mr. Barnes!" Her favorite teacher at Central was unlocking the front door of the house across the street.

"Who's Mr. Barnes?" asked Ruby.

"One of my teachers. And he's the advisor for our book club. I guess he lives here, right across from Aunt Allie — the person who started our summer book club. Isn't that a coincidence?"

"All right, girls," said Min. "Mind what Aunt Allie tells you tonight, remember your manners, and have fun. I'll see you tomorrow."

Flora and Ruby scrambled out of the car and ran to

the front door. "Isn't it cool that we have our very own room here?" said Flora.

"Yes," replied Ruby. She paused. "I do wonder about the food, though. What do you think we'll be eating?"

"I don't know," said Flora in a hurried whisper as she heard her aunt turn the doorknob, "but I packed four candy bars and a package of cookies, just in case."

"Good thinking," Ruby whispered back.

It turned out that — surprise — they needn't have worried. Aunt Allie had made a regular salad and prepared macaroni and cheese and hot dogs. "Everything is organic," she said. "And the hot dogs are really chicken dogs, but I promise you won't be able to tell the difference."

For dessert there was ice cream.

"Yum," said Flora later, patting her stomach as she pushed her empty bowl across the table.

"Double yum," said Ruby. "That was great. Thank you."

"Yes, thank you," said Flora.

"You're very welcome," replied Aunt Allie. "Okay. Ruby, Min said you need to take a shower tonight. Why don't you do that now? I'll show you where everything is."

It was while Ruby was taking her shower and Flora and her aunt were curled up in armchairs in the living room that Flora — to her surprise — found herself saying, "Aunt Allie? How much do you know about old people?"

Allie smiled. "What do you mean?"

Flora laced her fingers together. "Nikki said she didn't know that old people could date. And then I started wondering how often old people get married."

"Are you thinking about Min and Rudy Pennington?"

Flora nodded.

"Well, people can get married at any age. I suppose it's less likely to happen as they get older, but it does happen. I'm not sure that Min and Rudy are ready for that yet. But if they were, what would you think, Flora?"

"I'd think . . ." Flora chose her words carefully. She started over. "I love Mr. Pennington. And I love Min, of course. But I'm not sure . . . I'm not sure . . ."

"Are you not sure you want to share Min with anyone?"

Flora let out her breath. "Not yet, anyway."

"You and Ruby have been through an awful lot of changes in the last couple of years," said Allie. "Maybe you're simply not ready for another change, good or bad."

"Well, that makes more sense than thinking I was a mean person who didn't want Min to get married. I do want her to be happy," said Flora.

"I know you do," replied Aunt Allie. "But anyway, I

think Min and Mr. Pennington are a long way from marriage."

Ruby, wearing a flannel nightgown Flora had made for her, bounced into the living room then, wet hair glistening. "All done!" she announced.

"Good," said Allie briskly. "I think I'll take my shower now." She got to her feet. "Oh, I just remembered — I meant to put a night-light in your room. Do you think you'll want a night-light?"

"Well . . ." said Flora.

"Possibly," said Ruby.

Aunt Allie smiled. "There's a spare one in the linen closet."

"I know where that is," said Ruby.

Flora followed Ruby and their aunt upstairs. Allie disappeared into her bathroom, and Ruby continued down the hall. "Right here," she said, and flung open a door. Flora and Ruby stared at the items on the shelves.

"Whoa," said Flora.

And Ruby said, "Well, *this* is a surprise. I guess I opened the wrong door."

"I'll say," said Flora. "What *is* all this?" She glanced over her shoulder. The door to Allie's bathroom was closed.

"Baby stuff," replied Ruby in a low voice.

Flora looked at a shelf filled with unopened packages of infant clothes — lace-edged rompers and floral T-shirts and tiny embroidered socks and knitted caps and dresses and sleepers and soft pink shoes. Below was a shelf full of supplies — bottles and teething rings and receiving blankets and a set of brightly colored plastic keys and a number of things Flora couldn't identify. "It's all brand-new," she whispered.

Ruby let out a muffled squeal. "Aunt Allie's pregnant! We're going to get a cousin!"

But Flora shook her head. "No. I don't think so. Look, the clothes are all for a girl. How could she know she was having a girl?"

"She must have had that test done."

Flora shook her head again. "Nope. You can't have it done until you're several months pregnant. Remember when Mrs. Fong found out about Grace? She was definitely already pregnant then. You could tell just by looking at her. Aunt Allie is not pregnant. At least, not that pregnant."

"Well, maybe she just wants a girl really, really badly."

"But that doesn't make any sense. Why go out and buy all this stuff now when she might have a boy?"

"It's not *all* for a girl," said Ruby.

"The clothes are," Flora replied. "Look at all the lace and flowers. Not to mention the dresses. And those shoes. Anyway, this stuff has been around a while. Some of the packages are dusty." Flora drew her fingers across a package containing a pink-and-white-striped sleeper, then wiped her hand on her jeans.

"Well, this is just . . . weird," said Ruby.

"Girls?" called Aunt Allie.

And in a flash, Flora shut the door to the closet and pulled Ruby into their bedroom.

"Not a word, Ruby, not a word," exclaimed Flora softly. And she made her sister pinkie swear.

Surprise, surprise, thought Flora.

CHAPTER 21

Saturday, September 20th

"Please, please can't I go with you? Please, please, puh-*lease*?" cried Mae.

"Not this time," Nikki replied patiently. "This is a trip just for Flora and Ruby and Olivia and me."

"But I got dressed for Davidson's," said Mae, and Nikki could tell that her sister wasn't far from tears. "Look at me. Don't I look a little like a farmer?" Mae was wearing jeans and a blue-and-white-checked shirt.

"I suppose," replied Nikki. She was tempted to remark that no one had asked Mae to get dressed for Davidson's and that this particular behavior was a bit manipulative, but of course she said no such thing. "Mae, this is another one of our Saturday adventures. And Saturday adventures are just for —"

"I know. You don't have to say it again. They're just

for you and Olivia and Ruby and Flora. But that's not fair!"

"Mae," said Mrs. Sherman as Nikki edged toward the front door, "I know you want to go with Nikki, but you simply can't. For one thing, Nikki is riding her bicycle to Davidson's, and you're not allowed to do that. Anyway, sometimes Nikki does things just with her friends. And sometimes you do things just with yours. Besides, you and I are going to have fun today."

"What are we going to do? Clean?"

"Mae," said her mother warningly, and Nikki slipped out the door. She hoped her sister would be in a better frame of mind by the time she returned.

Nikki hopped on her bicycle. She rode carefully to the end of her lane, which was not paved and was peppered with holes and stones, then turned right on the county road where she picked up speed. She pedaled along, the air cool on her cheeks, the sun warming the top of her head. When she reached the intersection with the billboard advertising Davidson's Orchards, she parked her bike and was about to sit on a rock at the side of the road to wait for her friends when she heard a shout and saw Ruby, Flora, and Olivia riding toward her.

"Hi!" she called.

"Hi!" Ruby replied. "Get back on your bike!"

Nikki did so, and the four girls turned onto

Newtown-Pennswood Road. Every so often they passed another sign for Davidson's until finally Ruby said, "How much farther? I can't wait. This is going to be so much fun — hayrides, pony rides, a corn maze. I've never been in a corn maze."

"I've been going to Davidson's since I was little," said Olivia, puffing as she rode along. "Every year it gets bigger. First it was just a farm stand, then they added the pony rides, then apple picking."

"Now there's a general store, too," said Nikki. "And this year, I think there's a display of scarecrows."

"Here's the entrance," Olivia called over her shoulder.

The girls turned into a small parking lot and chained their bikes to a rack.

Ruby began jumping up and down. "Oh! Oh! A carousel! No one told me there would be a merry-go-round!"

"That's new," said Nikki slowly, and a very strange feeling came over her. She looked at the merry-go-round, which was noisy and festive, the horses colorful, the brass rings gleaming. She looked at Ruby's beaming face — and then she looked at the people riding the merry-go-round. They were all either parents or very young children. And suddenly Nikki felt she was much too old to ride the carousel. She recalled, with great discomfort, the December three years earlier when her mother had taken her and Mae to see the Santa Claus at the department store in the mall, and Nikki had realized in one great disappointing instant that she was the oldest kid in line. Without a word, she had stepped away, leaving her mother to settle Mae on Santa's lap, and had watched from the sidelines.

"Nikki? What's the matter?" asked Ruby now. "Come on. Olivia and Flora are already at the entrance."

Ruby pulled Nikki's arm and they joined a line of jostling, laughing people. When they passed through the gate, they found themselves in an autumn wonderland. Along the pathways through the farm were sheaves of cornstalks surrounded by enormous pumpkins. Food stalls featured donuts and caramel popcorn and hot chocolate, apple pie and apple cider and jars of homemade applesauce.

"Look, there are the scarecrows," said Flora.

The girls walked down a lane of scarecrows dressed as witches and monsters and princesses. "There's Peter Pan," said Olivia. "Oh, and the White Rabbit."

"It's like a costume parade for scarecrows," said Flora.

"Let's get a bag of popcorn," said Ruby. "One big bag for us to share."

The girls purchased their popcorn from a man dressed as a mummy and ambled through Davidson's. They watched a group of people leave on a hayride, inquired about apple picking, and wandered through the general store, paying close attention to an array of penny candy.

"Let's go through the corn maze," said Olivia. "It's really fun. It's huge, but you can't get lost because there are all these people in costumes who help you out if you get stuck."

"And then let's ride the merry-go-round," said Ruby.

Nikki glanced at Olivia and Flora and saw the same uncertainty on their faces that she had felt earlier.

"What?" asked Ruby. "No one wants to ride the merry-go-round?"

"Well . . ." said Flora.

"You think it's babyish, don't you?" said Ruby, sounding defiant. "What about a pony ride? Is that babyish, too?"

After a brief silence, Nikki said, "I don't think a hayride would be babyish. Or apple picking."

"Yeah. There's still plenty to do," said Olivia.

Nikki was aware of a rift between Ruby and the rest of them. Not a great one — not a chasm or a gulf — but something subtle and unpleasant that separated younger from older. And she realized that she didn't necessarily want to be on the older side. But there she was.

"Come on. I'll race you guys to the maze!" shouted Flora then, and Nikki and her friends took off running. Along the way, they passed a ring with four ponies plodding around and around, each ridden by a nervously happy child. Ruby looked longingly at the ponies. And Nikki thought, I'll come back here. I'll come back to Davidson's with Mae and she can ride a pony and the carousel and I'll watch her, just like I watched her sit in Santa's lap. It will be almost as much fun.

CHAPTER 22

Sunday, September 21st

Homework time was sacred to Olivia. She cherished it and she guarded it. This year, because she had so much homework, she had made a sign that she hung on her closed bedroom door whenever she was studying. The sign read WOMAN AT WORK. Olivia's parents and brothers knew not to disturb her when the sign was displayed.

On Sunday evening, Olivia, door closed, was seated in front of her computer, working on a composition titled "Why I Like Dogs." Olivia was more than competent at writing, but it didn't come as easily to her as other subjects did. Plus, because Olivia did not have a dog, she was having a bit of difficulty with the assignment. This wasn't a topic she would have chosen for herself. She had, in fact, drawn it out of a hat during English class on Friday, and she hadn't been able to trade for a different topic. As each student had pulled a slip of paper from the hat, he or she had been asked to read the topic aloud, and Mr. Barnes had kept a list of students and their topics. Jacob — lucky Jacob — had drawn a piece of paper with the words "Dreams and Nightmares" on it. He had confessed to Olivia at lunch that day that he wished he had chosen Olivia's subject. "Oh, and *I* wish I had chosen *yours*," she had assured him.

Now here she was, thinking about dogs she knew, and the people who owned them, and why *they* liked the dogs, and attempting to make the whole subject interesting and maybe even a bit funny. She was trying to finish a sentence she had started with — "I think dogs have a sense of humor because" — when she heard a knock at her door.

"Hello! The sign is hanging!" called Olivia.

"I know. I'm sorry," she heard Henry reply. "But there's a phone call for you. It's that girl Melody again. I told her about your sign and she's *still* on the phone. I'd hang up, but I already did that once and she called back."

Olivia heaved an annoyed sigh. "That's okay, Henry." She got up from her desk and opened her door. She was about to add "Melody is a major pain," when she realized that Henry was holding the phone out to her. Olivia put her hand over the mouthpiece. "Did Melody hear what you just said?" she hissed.

Henry shrugged. "I don't know."

Olivia took the phone into her room and closed the door behind her. She felt her heart begin to pound, and she drew in a deep breath. She had done Melody's science homework for her on Tuesday and her math homework for her in Thursday's study period, and she had fielded phone calls from her on Wednesday and Friday nights. Olivia had hoped not to hear from her again until at least Monday, but now Melody was on the phone and Olivia felt like a trapped animal.

She let her breath out and put the phone to her ear. "Hello?"

"Why didn't you talk to me when I called before?" was Melody's reply.

"I didn't know you had called. My brother didn't tell me." Olivia added, "My family knows I don't like to be disturbed when I'm doing my homework."

Olivia heard a noise at the other end of the phone that she couldn't quite identify. A snort? A laugh?

"Well, all I need is ten minutes of your pre — of your time," said Melody.

"Okay . . ."

"Tell me the answers to the science questions."

"Excuse me?"

"All right, *please* tell me the answers to the science questions."

Olivia's stomach took on an unpleasant hollow feeling. There were so many, many things wrong with what Melody was demanding of her. Olivia suddenly saw them all clearly, as if someone had listed them on a blackboard for her:

> Melody is using Olivia.
> By using Olivia, Melody is cheating.
> Therefore, Olivia is cheating, too.
> Melody is cutting into Olivia's homework time.
> Olivia's teachers are going to figure out what's
>   happening.

The list went on and on, but Olivia was jerked back to reality when she heard Melody say sweetly, "I *said* 'please.'"

"Sorry. I was just thinking. Melody . . . the answer is no."

"What?"

"The answer is no. I can't tell you the answers to the questions. In fact, I can't help you with your homework anymore. Not at school and not over the phone."

"Olivia, that really is not very nice. I think you're being awfully selfish. We're friends. You're smart. I need help. That's all there is to it."

"Well, actually," said Olivia, "I think there's another way to look at the problem. You should be getting help from our teachers or from a tutor, not from me. Last year, when my brother Jack needed help with his reading, my parents talked to his teacher and they found a tutor for him. He saw the tutor twice a week for —"

"Are you kidding?" interrupted Melody.

"What?"

"You're really not going to help me?"

"Melody, this isn't 'help.' What we're doing is . . . cheating."

"So?"

"*So?* So I'm not going to do it anymore." Olivia paused, then said what she had wanted to say to Melody five days earlier. "And you can't make me."

There was such a long silence from Melody's end of the line that Olivia actually held the phone out and shook it. When she put it to her ear again, she heard Melody saying, " . . . going to regret this. Because you're right, I can't make you do my work. But I can make you wish we never had this conversation." Olivia said nothing. "Olivia? Are you still there?"

"Yeah."

"Do you want to change your mind?"

"No."

"Okay. Whatever happens, remember what you said to me tonight . . . *friend*."

The line went dead. Olivia pressed the OFF button and let the phone slip onto her bed.

"Uh-oh," she whispered.

CHAPTER 23

Monday, September 22ⁿᵈ

The moment Nikki stepped off the school bus on Monday morning and caught sight of Olivia and Flora, who were waiting for her near the bicycle racks, she sensed trouble.

"Hi," she called to them. "What's wrong?"

"How can you tell something's wrong?" asked Flora.

"Your faces. You look like you just glimpsed, um," (Nikki tried to conjure up an appropriate image) "death," she finished.

Flora smiled, but Olivia remained solemn.

"Come on," said Nikki. "Tell me."

Olivia sat down heavily on one of the bike racks. "Melody called last night. She wanted me to help her again —"

"She didn't just want help," interrupted Flora. "She wanted Olivia to give her all the answers to their science assignment. Just *give* them to her."

"And I said no," Olivia continued. "I said I wasn't going to help her anymore. If you can call it help. Not over the phone and not in school."

"But that's great!" exclaimed Nikki.

Olivia shook her head. "I don't think so. Melody said I was going to regret it."

"What's she going to do? Tell the teachers you won't cheat?"

"She could tell them I *already* cheated. And you know she's going to tell her friends about last night. They can make things difficult for me. I don't know exactly what Melody is going to do, but she's going to do something."

"We'll protect you," said Nikki.

"Thanks," replied Olivia. "Maybe I should get a bodyguard," she added as a towering upperclassman brushed by them.

"You're coming to the meeting this afternoon, aren't you?" asked Nikki.

"What?" said Olivia, her mind on Melody. "Oh, yeah. The book club meeting. Yeah, I'll be there."

"Hey!" exclaimed Flora. "You know what I forgot to tell you guys? I found out that Mr. Barnes lives across the street from Aunt Allie."

"No way," said Nikki.

"Yup. I saw him going into his house when Min drove Ruby and me over there."

"Cool," said Nikki. "I think he's my favorite teacher."

"Mine, too," said Flora.

"Mine, too," said Olivia.

Nikki found it difficult to concentrate in school that day. She was mad at Melody, on Olivia's behalf. She spent some time worrying about what sort of revenge Melody might try to exact. Then her mind drifted to the meeting that afternoon — the first actual meeting of the book club — and she wondered if it would be a success. What if no one showed up? Well, that was silly. Nikki knew that plenty of kids were planning to attend. Her thoughts returned to Melody. And revenge.

When school ended that day, Nikki slammed her locker shut and went off in search of Olivia and Flora. She caught up with Olivia outside the door to Mr. Barnes's room. "How was your afternoon?" she asked her. "Did anything happen? Hey, look how many kids are here!"

"Nothing happened," replied Olivia. "Wow, this is great, Nikki."

Every seat in the classroom was already taken, and more kids were squeezing onto windowsills and lining up along the back wall. Nikki saw Claudette and Mary Louise and Jacob.

Olivia sighed. "No Melody or Tanya, thank goodness," she whispered.

Mr. Barnes clapped his hands then, and Nikki hurried to the back of the room, followed by Olivia and, a few moments later, Flora.

"So," began Mr. Barnes, smiling, "this is a great turnout. I'm glad to see all of you here. I've been doing a lot of thinking about the book club, and I've decided that while I will act as your advisor and be on hand at each meeting to give you guidance and answer questions, you should run the club yourselves. And that's what we need to talk about today: how the club will work. How will you select the books you'll read? How often will you meet? What will you do at meetings?" He spread his hands wide. "So. Any thoughts? Let's start with book selection. How will you do that?"

Jacob raised his hand. "We could take turns choosing the books."

"We could nominate a few books each month and vote on one," said Mary Louise.

"Can we choose any book at all, or does it have to be, like, age appropriate?" asked a boy sitting on a windowsill.

Flora raised her hand and said timidly, "Are we only going to read fiction, or could we choose a biography or poetry or something?"

At that point, everyone began to talk at once, and Mr. Barnes held up his hand like a police officer stopping a car at an intersection. Nikki thought he was going to ask for quiet, but all he said was, "There's a lot to think about, isn't there? Let's go back to the selection process. I heard one suggestion for taking turns choosing and one for voting at each meeting. Thoughts?"

Jacob raised his hand again. "I just realized something. There are thirty-four of us here, and even if we met every two weeks — which is probably too often — not everyone would get a turn to choose a book by the end of the year. So maybe voting is a better idea."

"What do the rest of you think?" asked Mr. Barnes.

There was general consent, and then a girl in the front row said, "How are we going to nominate the books, though? We can't *each* nominate one. That doesn't make any sense."

The discussion continued. When Mr. Barnes said, "We'd better wrap things up in ten minutes," Nikki looked at the clock on the wall and couldn't believe how much time had gone by. She had thoroughly enjoyed the meeting and was pleased with the decisions that had been reached: to meet once a month; to open each meeting with a discussion of the book that had just been read; to then break into groups of four or five, each group being responsible for nominating one title; to vote on the new book by the end of the meeting; to be able to read all kinds of books; and (this was Mr. Barnes's suggestion) to consider having two book-related field trips each year. They planned to meet again on the following Monday in order to choose their first book.

"This is going to be *so cool!*" exclaimed Nikki as she left Mr. Barnes's room with Flora, Olivia, Claudette, and Jacob.

"I can't wait —" Olivia started to say and then stopped short.

"What?" said Claudette.

"Nothing," muttered Olivia.

Nikki followed Olivia's gaze and caught sight of Melody and Tanya down the hall. They were watching the kids stream out of the classroom.

"Ha!" exclaimed Flora. "Melody doesn't look too happy about how many kids went to the meeting. She thought the club was a stupid idea."

Nikki turned to Olivia who, eyes averted from Melody, was now looking over a book list with Jacob. "Huh," said Nikki. "I have a feeling that's not the only thing she's unhappy about."

CHAPTER 24

Tuesday, September 23rd

Olivia had half expected to get a phone call from Melody on Monday night — one final demand for help — but the call didn't come. In fact, the phone rang only twice that evening, both times for Mrs. Walter. Maybe, thought Olivia as she slid under her covers and turned out her reading light, the incident with Melody was over. She had a strong suspicion that Melody wouldn't speak to her again, which was fine with her. But revenge? Melody was probably bluffing. After all, this was just plain old Central in plain old Camden Falls, not a made-for-TV movie. Or perhaps Melody's revenge was simply to leave Olivia *expecting* revenge — dreading every ring of the phone, wondering what was around every corner, both literally and figuratively. Ha, thought Olivia. She had trumped Melody, figured her out. Revenge by no revenge. That was fairly lame. But when would Olivia know that no revenge was ever going to be forthcoming? In a week? A month? By the end of the school year? And that, she realized bleakly, was the beauty of such a heavily veiled threat.

"Did you hear anything from Melody?" Flora asked Olivia as they hurried down Main Street the next morning.

Olivia peered longingly into the window of Cover to Cover, which featured a display of books about mammals. "I wish I knew more about skeletons," she remarked. She turned back to Flora. "Melody? Nope. Not a word. I don't think she's going to call again." Olivia didn't add that Melody's very silence may have indicated the brilliance of her revenge.

"Aren't you sort of wondering what's going to happen?" asked Flora.

"Mm. Let's not talk about it."

Olivia and Flora reached Central early enough to meet Nikki's bus. The three friends chatted outside and finally made their way through the front entrance. "See you!" they called to one another.

Olivia ran to the second floor. At her locker, she put on her usual show of twisting the dial around and around. She had made up a pretend combination for the lock — 8-19-41 — and hoped that she appeared wonderfully casual and nonchalant as she turned the knob once to the right, then twice around in the other direction, then to the right again, carefully stopping at 41. Bingo! her hands seemed to say as, with a flourish, she pulled the door open. Olivia stashed all but two of her books on the shelf. Then she placed her completed homework assignments in a special folder (labeled, appropriately, HOMEWORK), laid the folder on top of the books, closed her locker, and, just to complete the show, twisted the useless dial several times before hurrying down the hall.

She had not so much as glimpsed Melody.

Later that morning, Olivia stopped by her locker to switch books and to pick up her homework assignments for her next two classes. She grabbed a notebook and her science text, then opened the folder.

Olivia had placed her assignments in the HOME-WORK folder in the order in which she would need them. Her science paper (Miss Allen's assignment the previous day had been to answer eight questions about the periodic table of elements) should now have been on the top. It wasn't. Strange that it was out of order. Olivia shuffled through the other pages in the folder. No science assignment. Where could it be? She had spent an hour on it the night before and she distinctly remembered putting it in the folder that morning. Panic rising, she knelt on the floor and shuffled through her notebook, then paged through the science book. Nothing and nothing. The bell was about to ring again.

Olivia scrabbled through every book in the locker and shoved aside an umbrella and a jacket she'd forgotten about, but found no assignment.

And then, in that strange way that thoughts have of jumping into your mind, she saw with great clarity exactly what had happened to her assignment. Melody must have figured out, probably days and days ago, that Olivia couldn't lock her locker, and she had simply opened it sometime that morning, located the assignment (Olivia now regretted the boldly labeled folder), and removed it. If she had done that early enough in the morning, she would have had time to copy it over in her own writing. So. Melody had found a way to get science assignments out of Olivia after all. And Olivia now had no work of her own to hand in.

So much for the theory of revenge by no revenge.

Somewhat to her surprise, Olivia discovered that she was angry rather than frightened. She practically stomped all the way to her science class. By the time she reached the door, she had decided several things: 1. She was not going to tell on Melody, mainly because she couldn't prove what had happened, but also because she had a fuzzily formed suspicion that it would be better not to let on that she had figured out what Melody was up to. 2. Rather than appear upset in class, she was simply going to tell Miss Allen that she must have left her work at home and ask if she could hand it in the next day. 3. She was going to get revenge of her own on Melody. She didn't know how she was going to accomplish this, but with the help of Nikki, Flora, and Ruby, she knew she would find a way.

Olivia entered her science classroom and walked to her desk. As soon as she sat down, she began to page through her books as though searching for her assignment, which she had just discovered was not in its folder. When Miss Allen said, "Homework, please," Olivia raised her hand.

"Yes, Olivia?"

"I'm really sorry, but I can't find mine." Olivia didn't dare look in Melody's direction. "I did the work, and I thought I brought it to school, but I guess I left it at home. Could I hand it in tomorrow?"

Miss Allen bestowed a look of great suspicion upon her star student but granted her an extension of one day.

"Thank you," said Olivia meekly.

"Oh, my stars," said Flora, when Olivia told her and Nikki about the missing assignment in the cafeteria that day. "What are you going to do? What about the rest of your homework?"

"Don't worry," Olivia replied. "I'm carrying it with me. I'm carrying all my important stuff with me." She rubbed her shoulder. "My backpack weighs a ton, though. I might as well be carrying a suitcase. But I am not," she said vehemently, "going to let Melody get the better of me."

"Really?" Nikki regarded Olivia with interest. "What are you planning? I know you're planning something."

"Revenge of my own," said Olivia. "I don't know what it's going to be, but I'll come up with something." She paused. "Will you guys help me? You and Ruby?"

"Of course," said Flora. "This afternoon?"

Olivia shook her head. "I'll have to do all my homework, plus *re*do the science assignment. How about tomorrow?"

"We're there," said Flora. "I'll tell Ruby."

And Nikki added, "Gosh, Olivia, you look sort of . . . I've never seen you . . . I mean, you don't look upset, you look . . ."

"Mad?" suggested Olivia.

"Yeah," said Nikki.

"Well, I am. And Melody is going to regret it."

"Cool," said Nikki.

CHAPTER 25

Wednesday, September 24ᵗʰ

Nikki spent much of Tuesday evening thinking of ways for Olivia to get back at Melody. After she had finished her homework, she'd turned to a fresh page in her notebook and written across the top REVENGE 101. Although she couldn't come up with anything to list on the page, she did recall a saying about revenge, and she scribbled *Revenge is a dish best served cold* below the heading. She stared at the page for a while and then finally put her notebook away. She hoped her mind would be more fertile the next day.

"Okay, you guys. Where shall we meet?" Nikki asked Olivia and Flora as they walked down Main Street after school on Wednesday.

"My room, I suppose," replied Olivia.

But when Ruby caught up with them a few minutes

later, she said, "We never meet in my room. Can't we meet in my room today? I want to have the revenge meeting there."

"Sure," said Olivia.

The girls settled themselves in Ruby's room. Daisy Dear joined them, first lolling on her back, inviting Nikki to rub her belly, and then rolling over and resting her giant head in Nikki's lap.

"It's hard to think about revenge with a dog's head in your lap," commented Nikki. "Look at Daisy's kind eyes. I bet dogs never think about revenge."

"Nope. Just about squirrels," replied Ruby. "Okay. Let's get cracking."

"Well," Nikki began, and was about to tell the others that she didn't seem to be very adept at plotting revenge, when she was interrupted by Ruby.

"Okay." Ruby snapped her chewing gum. Then, with a flourish, she shook open a piece of paper. "Here's what I came up with: One, sneak into the girls' bathroom and wrap one of the toilets with cellophane. When Melody sits on it, well, you can imagine what happens."

"Um," said Olivia. "I don't —"

"*Two*," Ruby continued loudly, "trip her in the hallway with everyone watching, especially that boy Jacob." She glanced at Olivia, then returned to her paper. "Three, sneak a fly or a spider into her food at lunchtime. Four —"

"Ruby?" said Nikki. There was something — no, there were many things — that made Ruby's suggestions difficult to carry out. For instance, how could Olivia be sure Melody and not someone else would sit on the toilet? And how exactly was Olivia supposed to sneak a fly into Melody's food? But Nikki didn't want to hurt Ruby's feelings. She thought for a moment and said, "Those are good suggestions, but I think the perfect revenge should involve homework. Melody is getting back at Olivia for refusing to help her, so Olivia has to hit Melody where it hurts — in her homework."

"*Oh*," said Ruby, tapping her temple with her forefinger. "Very clever."

"Yeah," said Nikki. "It's a clever thought; I just didn't come up with any actual ideas." She stroked Daisy's sleeping head.

Flora squinted her eyes and stared at the ceiling.

Olivia, who was sitting at Ruby's desk, put her chin in her hand. "Hmm."

"You could steal Melody's homework," Ruby said to Olivia.

"But how?" asked Olivia. "I'll bet Melody doesn't have a broken lock on her locker. Anyway, I don't want to stoop to her level."

"You *have* to get your lock fixed, Olivia," said Flora.

"I know."

"So far," said Ruby, sounding vaguely annoyed, "I'm the only one coming up with any ideas."

"Well, give me a minute," said Olivia. "I *am* thinking."

"Me, too," said Nikki and Flora.

Ruby's room became very quiet.

"You know," said Olivia slowly, "I might be able to use the broken lock to my advantage."

"What do you mean?" asked Ruby.

"Well . . . Melody doesn't know that I know that she knows the lock is broken."

"*If* she knows," said Flora. "I mean, if she actually did take your homework."

"Oh, she did. I'm sure of it. Miss Allen handed back Monday's assignment this morning — and Melody got a one hundred. You should have seen the look on Miss Allen's face. I'm pretty certain Melody got the hundred because she copied my missing paper. Anyway, what I was going to say is that Melody doesn't know I've figured out what's going on. She thinks that I think I just lost the assignment. So . . . Melody is going to feel free to raid my locker again."

"Well, duh," said Ruby. "I thought that was the whole point of this meeting."

"I *know*," said Olivia. "But here's the thing: We *have* figured out what's going on. Now, how can we use that little bit of knowledge?"

Nikki almost laughed but ducked her head instead and stroked Daisy, who apparently was having an exciting dream.

"You could write Melody a note telling her how stupid she is," said Ruby, "and leave it in your locker for her to find the next time she breaks in."

"Hey!" exclaimed Olivia, jumping out of the chair. "You're brilliant, Ruby!"

"She is?" said Flora. "You're going to write Melody a note telling her she's stupid?"

"No. But I'm going to plant fake homework assignments in the folder."

"What do you mean, 'fake' assignments?" asked Nikki with interest.

"I mean," replied Olivia, looking faintly devilish, "that I'm going to do the homework all wrong. Then Melody will copy it, hand it in, and get a D — or an F!"

"But Melody isn't going to keep copying your assignments if she gets D's and F's," said Ruby.

"Exactly," said Olivia. "She'll quit stealing from me. This only has to happen once. And when Melody sees that I not only handed in the assignment, too, but that I got an A on it, she'll know I knew what she was up to. And then she can sit around wondering if I'm going to tell any of our teachers about it."

"Oh, this is perfect!" cried Flora.

"It's great," agreed Nikki. "But how can you be sure when Melody is going to raid your locker again, Olivia?"

"I can't. I'll have to . . ." Olivia paused, thinking. "I guess I'll have to make two copies of all the assignments for the classes Melody and I have together — one correct copy for me and one fake copy for Melody. Then, let me see . . . I'll put Melody's copies in the folder in my locker for her to steal, and I'll carry my own copies around in my backpack. I'll have to keep checking my locker to see if Melody has broken into it. And the next time an assignment is missing, I'll hand my own copy in secretly, if I can. You know — so Melody won't suspect anything until later, when the assignment is handed back. And then she'll get a real surprise. This will be a lot of work, but it'll be worth it."

"I like everything about your plan, Olivia," said Flora, "except . . . aren't you nervous about what Melody will do to get back at *you*? I mean, this could go on forever."

"But I don't think it will," said Olivia, chin thrust forward. "I'll get my locker fixed, like I said, and anyway, I don't care. I have my friends. If we have to get back at Melody again, you'll help me; I know that. Eventually, Melody will give up. She can't beat us. We're too strong."

"United we stand," said Nikki. "All right. Let's get started on fake assignments."

CHAPTER 26

Thursday, September 25ᵗʰ

Min Read stood in the living room of the Row House and looked out onto Aiken Avenue. How many times, she wondered, had she stood in this same spot and looked out at this same section of the street? Thousands and thousands, she guessed. When she was a very little girl, she would kneel on the couch — a fancy, many pillowed, blue-and-white couch that had come from a store on Main Street called...Clancy's? No, Clement's. She would kneel backward on the couch from Clement's, her chin in her hands, and look at the house across the street, a gracious old home that was older than the Row Houses. Min's friend Doris had lived there. Doris was a pudgy, serious girl who wore round glasses and sat on her front porch, eating chocolates and reading one book after another. What had become of Doris? Min wondered. Doris had moved away and Min had never heard from her. Another family had bought the house, a family with three boys, and then *they* had moved away.

Funny what one remembered, thought Min, when one's mind was drifting. She now recalled the years when she was a parent of two young girls and a new group of families lived in the Row Houses and on Aiken Avenue. Nearly every morning at a quarter past ten, Min would step out her back door and wait for Josie Reese, the mother of Olivia's mother, Wendy, to appear on her stoop. Min and Josie would raise invisible coffee mugs in the air and then Josie would cross the yards to Min's house, or Min would cross the yards to Josie's (depending on whose turn it was to make the coffee), and they would chat for half an hour or so before getting back to their mornings.

And how many times had they done *that*? Min wondered. Hundreds, she supposed, or thousands, and now Josie lived outside of Camden Falls, and Wendy was all grown up and had three children of her own, and Min was raising two granddaughters.

"Min?"

Min jumped at the sound of Flora's voice.

"Is everything all right? I thought I heard you sigh."

"Just recalling old times," said Min.

"Good old times?" asked Flora.

"Yes."

"Sometimes good old times seem sad later. I mean,

because they were so good before and now they're over and you long for them."

"You are much too young to be having such thoughts, honey," said Min.

"What *were* you thinking about?" said Flora. "If it's okay to ask."

"Well, first I was remembering who lived in the house across the street when I was a little girl."

"And who did live there?"

"Several families, but the Stevensons are the ones I remember the best. There was a girl named Doris who always made me think of an old schoolmarm, even though she was exactly my age. When we played school she was always the teacher and her favorite thing was thinking up punishments for naughty students. Sometimes she made the smaller children cry. I think I was the only one who really liked her. She was always willing to share her candy with me."

"And what happened to Doris? Where does she live now?"

Min shook her head. "Don't know. My goodness, there have been a lot of changes on this street."

"Min? I don't like change," said Flora. She and Min sat down on the couch, and Flora rested her head on her grandmother's shoulder.

"Change in general?" asked Min. "Or do you mean something in particular?" Flora didn't answer. "Are you talking about your parents and your move here or about something more recent?"

"More recent."

"Do you mean Mr. Pennington and me?"

Min felt Flora's head nod against her shoulder, and Flora said in a rush, "I know I'm being selfish. I love you. I want you to be happy. And I know how much *your* life changed when Ruby and I came here. But what would happen if you and Mr. Pennington got married? Would he move in with us? Would —"

"Flora, wait," said Min, and she sat forward and turned to face her granddaughter. "We're a long way from marriage."

"But you're spending so much time together."

"Yes. We are. We've both been married, and we miss the companionship that comes with marriage. I feel lucky to have found it again with Rudy. We've been neighbors for a long, long time, so we know each other well. And lately, we've felt our friendship becoming something deeper. I'm very grateful for that."

"But what's going to happen?" asked Flora again.

"I'm afraid I can't tell you that. I don't have an answer. Right now, Rudy and I are just enjoying spending time together. And by the way, Rudy adores you and your sister. I hope you know that. He wants to be able to spend more time with the two of you."

"We love Mr. Pennington," said Flora.

"But?" Min prompted her, and Flora shrugged. "But you're just not ready for more change, is that it?"

"I guess so."

Min refrained from sighing again. At least, she thought, the problem was out in the open.

CHAPTER 27

Friday, September 26th

At lunchtime on Friday, Flora stood waiting by the entrance to the cafeteria and was soon greeted by a jubilant Olivia.

"What?" asked Flora, smiling. "What is it?"

"My math homework disappeared!" Olivia looked up and down the hall and then lowered her voice. "I just checked my locker and the fake math paper I put in the folder this morning is gone," she whispered.

"Wow. Melody didn't waste any time striking again, did she?"

"She must think she's awfully clever," said Olivia.

Nikki joined them then. "What's going on?"

"Melody took my math homework," Olivia reported. "I mean, the fake math work. I put it in the folder as soon as I got to school. When I checked my locker just now, it wasn't there."

"You have your own copy of the assignment, though, don't you?" asked Nikki.

Olivia patted her backpack. "Right here. Now I just have to figure out how to hand it in this afternoon without Melody's seeing me. I don't want her to catch on and ask Mr. Krauss for her paper back."

"How does Mr. Krauss collect your work?" asked Flora.

"We just drop it on his desk when we come into the room."

"Well, that's easy, then. Get to class early and put your paper facedown on the desk before Melody even gets there."

"Oh! Oh!" exclaimed Nikki. "I just thought of a nice touch, Olivia. You could ask Mr. Krauss a question — about anything, really — and you could look really serious while he answers you. If Melody sees you having a serious discussion with him when she gets to class, she'll probably assume you're telling Mr. Krauss that you lost your homework. She won't have a clue!"

"That's perfect!" cried Flora. "We're very devious."

"Oh, I can't *wait* for Monday," said Olivia gaily as the girls entered the cafeteria.

"How did it go?" Flora asked Olivia the moment they met up after school.

They were standing by Olivia's locker, and Olivia shushed her and once again looked up and down the hall like a spy. "I don't want to spoil our plans," she whispered. "Not now."

"Okay. Sorry," Flora whispered back. "Hey, here comes Nikki."

Olivia refused to say a word about math class until the girls were standing on the front lawn of Central. At last, she said, "Okay. This is what happened: I rushed to Mr. Krauss's room as fast as I could and I was the first person there. Even Mr. Krauss hadn't arrived yet. I left my paper on his desk. Then a few more kids came in and they put their papers on top of mine, so it was buried. Then Mr. Krauss finally showed up and I saw that Melody was right behind him, so I went to the front of the room and I asked him a question about prime numbers. I really did have a question about them," she added. "Did you know that prime numbers —"

"Um, Olivia," Flora interrupted her, "could you skip the part about the prime numbers?"

"Thank you," Nikki whispered to Flora.

"Oh. Okay," said Olivia. "Well, Mr. Krauss's answer was kind of long, and I was having a little trouble following what he was saying, so I probably did appear very serious while we were talking, and after we finished, I turned around and saw Melody looking straight at me, and she was smirking. Smirking! Oh, this is so great."

Flora had rarely seen her friend in such a good mood. Olivia chattered all the way to Sincerely Yours for her Friday afternoon job, and when she entered the store, she was grinning.

Flora found herself grinning, too, and hummed a little tune on her way to the Row Houses. When Ruby came home, Flora gleefully reported Olivia's news to her.

"Wah-hoo!" cried Ruby. "Melody is *so* dead. She is *so* going to regret this. She is *so* going to be embarrassed. She is *so* —" The doorbell rang then, and Ruby cried guiltily, "What if that's Melody?"

"Oh, for heaven's sake," said Flora. She peeked out the front window. "It's Mr. Pennington."

Mr. Pennington, holding his hat in front of him in a gentlemanly fashion, stepped inside. "I was wondering —"

"Min's not home yet," interrupted Ruby.

"I was *wondering*," Mr. Pennington began again, "if I might escort you two lovely young ladies to the Marquis Diner for dinner tonight. Would you care to join me? I've already cleared it with Min."

Flora, correctly suspecting that Min had told Mr. Pennington about their conversation the day before, hesitated. But Ruby cried, "We can use our coupons for the free sandwiches! Won't that be fun? Then we'll only have to pay for, like, drinks and ice cream and stuff. We *can* have ice cream, can't we?"

"I don't see why not. How about if I pick you up at five-thirty?" said Mr. Pennington.

"We'll be all gussied up and ready to go," replied Ruby, quoting Min.

Mr. Pennington was punctual. The doorbell rang at exactly five-thirty, and Flora and Ruby, coupons in hand, were indeed ready to go.

Later, having turned in their coupons, Mr. Pennington and the Northrop sisters sat at a booth in the Marquis. Ruby was jealous because Hilary had shown them to the booth, and Ruby wanted a grown-up job of her own (although Hilary pointed out that she didn't get paid and didn't have actual hours, either).

"Tell me, Ruby, what's happening at Camden Falls Elementary this year?" said Mr. Pennington, and Flora was grateful for his attempt at distracting her.

Ruby brightened. "It's very interesting. We have a sister school." She told him about her pen pal and about Hilary's T-shirt design and various fund-raising activities.

"And you?" Mr. Pennington asked Flora. "How are things going at Central?"

Flora told him about Olivia and Melody and the devious plan.

Mr. Pennington laughed. "You know, when I was a little boy," he said, "I was once very upset because another boy kept copying my work. Right in class. But every time I complained to the teacher, the boy said *I* had been copying from *him*. And I couldn't prove otherwise, since of course our work was exactly the same."

"What did you do?" asked Flora, interested.

"Well, I was very pleased with myself," Mr. Pennington began. And he told them the rest of the story, and then about his family and his childhood, and later about the years when he was a teacher at Camden Falls Elementary.

By the time dinner was over, Flora felt as though she had a new grandfather.

CHAPTER 28

Saturday, September 27th

"It feels funny to be going to school on Saturday, doesn't it?" said Ruby. She and Hilary walked briskly along Dodds Lane, each carrying a bag from Camden Falls Art Supply.

"A little," agreed Hilary. "But fun, too." She patted her bag. "I got great stuff yesterday."

"Me, too. I'm glad Min knew there was a sale."

"I wonder how much money we'll raise at school today," said Hilary.

"I don't know, but probably a lot. There's the car wash and the raffle."

"The bake sale," added Hilary.

"And the sale of your T-shirts."

"Well, not *my* T-shirts."

"But with your design!" exclaimed Ruby. "It's very

cool." She tried to peek into Hilary's bag. "What did you buy?" she asked.

"Two boxes of crayons, a package of erasers, a package of pencils, and two wooden rulers. I wanted to buy a calculator, but I was spending my own money and I ran out. What did you buy?"

"Well, I had my own money plus some from Min," said Ruby, suddenly feeling a bit spoiled. "So I bought a pack of construction paper, some glue sticks, a package of markers, these pens that write in all different colors, and ten packs of stickers. I know you don't really need stickers or fancy pens for school, but, well, wouldn't you want to have something fun in your backpack?"

"Definitely," said Hilary.

Ruby was excited about the backpack project, in large part because her class had come up with the idea for it. They had been talking with Mrs. Caldwell about the William Jefferson Clinton Elementary School one morning, and Hilary had said, "It would be nice if our pen pals could get new supplies of their very own. It's great to raise money for supplies for the school, but my pen pal said she misses her backpack and all the stuff that was in her desk at her old home."

"Maybe," Ruby called out, "we could use some of the money we raise to buy backpacks for the kids."

"And we could *fill* the backpacks before we send them to Florida!" exclaimed Ava Longyear.

After some discussion, Ruby and her classmates had decided that during the autumn, the kids at CFE would collect brand-new school supplies, and then in December they would purchase backpacks, fill them with the supplies, and send them to Florida in time for the start of second semester.

Today was the first time supplies would be collected.

"You know," said Ruby, as she and Hilary approached school, "maybe at Halloween, instead of spending money on a class party, we could buy more supplies."

"That's a great idea!" said Hilary. "Tell Mrs. Caldwell about it today."

Ruby hefted her bag from one arm to the other. "Wow," she said. "Look how many people are already here."

She and Hilary slowed to a stop. Ahead of them, the school parking lot was crowded, and a line of cars was waiting to be washed and polished. Two tables had been set up by the front door and were laden with cakes, cookies, brownies, muffins, and pies.

"There's the T-shirt table," said Ruby. "It's *stacked* with your shirts. I'm definitely going to buy one. A red one, I think."

"I'm going to get a yellow one. Mom gave me ten dollars this morning. Where should we help out first?"

"Car wash," Ruby replied instantly. "After we give Mrs. Caldwell our supplies."

The girls hurried across the lawn to their teacher, who was standing by a bin marked BACKPACK SUPPLIES.

Ruby skidded to a halt. "Mrs. Caldwell! You're wearing blue jeans!"

Hilary nudged her friend. "*Ruby*," she hissed.

"Well, I've never seen her in jeans before," Ruby whispered back.

Mrs. Caldwell was smiling. "Thank you for your donations, girls. Put them right in there." She indicated the bin, which was already nearly half full.

Ruby placed her bag inside. "Notebooks, markers, pens," she said, eyeing the other donations. "Hey! Books! I mean, books to read for fun. This is great."

"People have been bringing things by all morning," said Mrs. Caldwell, smiling. "Mrs. Samson will be thrilled."

"Ruby," said Hilary, "tell Mrs. Caldwell your idea for the Halloween party."

Ruby did so, and Mrs. Caldwell beamed and said, "You can tell the class about this on Monday."

"Okay. We're going to help out at the car wash now," Ruby announced.

The car wash project had been organized by the sixth-graders. Ruby and Hilary approached a boy and two girls who looked as though they were in charge.

"What do you want us to do?" asked Ruby.

"You can keep the buckets filled with clean water," said one of the girls.

"Or wring out the dirty sponges," said the other girl.

"Or you can try to bring in more customers," said the boy.

"Oh! Oh! That's the job for me!" exclaimed Ruby.

"Um, I think I'll fill the buckets," said Hilary.

"See you," Ruby replied, and she ran to the middle of the parking lot, cupped her hands around her mouth, and shouted, "Attention! Attention, everyone! Is your car dirty? Is it dusty? Does it maybe smell? Then drive it to our car wash and have it cleaned. It will change your life! Come one, come all. And help out our pen pals in Florida."

As the afternoon drew to a close, Ruby looked at her watch. She had promised Min she'd be home half an hour from now, so she left her post in the parking lot and found Hilary, who was now helping with the bake sale.

"We'd better buy our T-shirts and get going," said Ruby.

Mrs. Caldwell drew Ruby aside. "Ruby," she said, "you were a true asset to the car wash. It's raised almost six hundred dollars so far."

"Thank you," said Ruby. She paused, then added modestly, "I have an extremely loud voice."

CHAPTER 29

Sunday, September 28th

Bill Willet put his hat on his head, stepped through his front door, locked it behind him, and stood on his stoop. He didn't like the sight of the FOR SALE sign in his yard. The seven letters on it spelled, for him, a tale of Alzheimer's, aging, change, and loss. Bill and Mary Lou had moved to the Row Houses when they were a young couple, and Mr. Willet had thought they would spend the rest of their lives here. He remembered the mornings, decades of mornings, sitting in the kitchen drinking coffee with Mary Lou, looking out the window at the bird feeder in the elm tree. One winter, a one-legged chickadee had come around and hung upside down from the branches while he ate sunflower seeds. Another year, a black squirrel had shown up. Mary Lou had liked him, even though he had hogged the feeder and kept the birds away, and she had scolded

Bill when he'd gone into town and returned from the hardware store with something called a squirrel baffle.

When Bill thought of leaving Aiken Avenue behind, he realized that what he would miss most were not holidays and milestones but ordinariness. He could recall walking through the front door at the end of a workday, building a fire in the fireplace on a chilly evening, sitting with Mary Lou in the back garden, and thousands and thousands of other simple moments in this house. He was glad he had had those moments and glad to have shared so many of them with Mary Lou, but he supposed he was a selfish man, because he wanted more.

Mr. Willet, cane in hand, made his way down the front path and turned onto the sidewalk. It was a dank and misty day, but his destination, the Edwardses', was close by. His Row House neighbors were giving him a good-bye party. Mr. Willet was grateful for this, but wished there was no reason for the party in the first place. Would he ever, he wondered, get used to arriving at parties alone, as he had done so easily when he was a single man, before Mary Lou had come into his life? Would he get used to invitations with only his name on the envelope?

As Mr. Willet was passing Min Read's house, Rudy Pennington opened his front door and waved. Mr. Willet waited for him on the sidewalk.

"Look at us," said Mr. Pennington. "Two old men with canes and hearing aids. Who would have thunk it? That's what my father used to say. 'Who would have thunk it?'"

Mr. Willet offered him a smile. "When I look in the mirror," he said, "I see an old man. But without the mirror I'm still the boy from Kalamazoo. I could be fifteen or ten. Or three."

"Is today a hard day?" asked Mr. Pennington. He took his old friend by the elbow and they turned up the Edwardses' walk.

"It's a bit of a sad day," said Mr. Willet.

"You know you'll have lots of visitors at Three Oaks, don't you? Min and I will come. And Flora. Flora likes going to Three Oaks. Plenty of other people —"

At that moment, Robby flung open the door. "Welcome!" he cried. "Here's our guest of honor! Everyone, the guest of honor is here! Mom! Dad! It's Mr. Willet! Oh, and Mr. Pennington."

Robby's mother greeted the men. "I wish we could have had nicer weather for the party," she said. "I thought we'd be outside this afternoon." She took their coats and ushered them into the living room.

Mr. Willet brightened. Here were Min and Flora and Ruby. Here were the Walters and the Morrises and the Malones. Here were the Fongs with Grace. A baby, thought Mr. Willet, was always a cheering sight. He turned back to Mrs. Edwards. "This is lovely," he said.

"No matter what the weather." And he offered her a genuine smile. "My goodness, look at all this food."

"We all brought something," said Ruby. "That's Min's artichoke dip in the green bowl." She stood on tiptoe and whispered in his ear, "If you don't like artichokes it's okay. Just say 'No, thank you' if someone passes you the bowl."

"I'll do that," replied Mr. Willet solemnly.

"Sit here, Bill," said Mr. Edwards, indicating an armchair by the fireplace. He had entered the room holding a large book. "This is the spot for our special guest."

Mr. Willet sat in the chair, and Mr. Edwards placed the book in his lap.

"What's this?" asked Mr. Willet.

Robby appeared at his side, bouncing up and down on his toes. "Look! Look at the cover. It says 'Row House Days.' The title was my idea. It's a scrapbook of —"

Robby's mother put a hand on his arm. "Wait. Let Mr. Willet open it and see for himself."

"Okay," said Robby, and he retreated a step but continued to bounce.

Mr. Willet opened the cover. On the first page was a photo of the Row Houses. Above it was written *Memories of Aiken Avenue*.

"Oh, my," said Mr. Willet. He pulled a handkerchief out of his pocket and blew his nose.

"Is he *crying*?" Ruby whispered to Lacey Morris. "Oh, no. He's crying."

Lacey nudged Ruby with her ankle. "*SHH.*"

Mr. Willet turned the page and there was a photo of Mary Lou in her wedding dress. Next to it was a black-and-white photo of three bridesmaids and three groomsmen standing in a loose semicircle. The women were wearing identical gowns and the men were wearing tuxes. *The Beginning* was written above the left-hand page.

"Where — where did —" Mr. Willet couldn't finish the sentence.

"We all contributed things," spoke up Dr. Malone.

"And not just photos," said Ruby. "There's all kinds of, um . . ."

"Memorabilia," supplied Olivia.

Mr. Willet turned to a page in the middle of the book. "Oh, my goodness!" he exclaimed. "Is this from that Fourth of July party?"

"What Fourth of July party?" asked Jack Walter.

"Your mother was just a little girl then," Mr. Willet told him. "We had a picnic in the backyards and your mother made a menu that she passed out to everyone. Here's the menu."

"Mom! You were not a very good speller," said Henry accusingly. "Look at that. It says 'corn on the cobe' and 'vegetabals' and 'lawyer cake.'"

"Nowadays we would call that inventive spelling," said Mrs. Walter with dignity.

Mr. Willet laughed. "Oh," he said, turning pages, "here's the Morrises' Christmas card from the year the twins were born. And here's a picture of Daisy Dear when she was a puppy. And newspaper headlines — what's this?"

"Remember when the hot-air balloon accidentally landed in the street?" said Mr. Pennington. "Aiken Avenue made the front page of the paper."

"Why, I haven't thought of that in years," said Mr. Willet.

For the next hour, the scrapbook was passed around and exclaimed over. The children asked questions and the grown-ups kept saying, "Remember when?" and "Remember this person?" And Mr. Willet, who had entered the Edwardses' house with a heavy heart, now felt much lighter.

"What a lovely gift," he said. "This will be the first thing I unpack at Three Oaks. Thank you very much."

"You're welcome," said Robby. "See? Now you'll have Aiken Avenue with you no matter where you are."

CHAPTER 30

Monday, September 29ᵗʰ

"I have butterflies in my stomach!" exclaimed Olivia. "*Butterflies.* As if I had to give a speech or be in a play or something."

"Are you sure you're going to get the homework back today?" asked Nikki.

Olivia, Nikki, and Flora stood in a huddle at the edge of the front lawn at Central.

"Well, pretty sure," Olivia replied. "We'd better. I don't think I can wait another day."

"Are you excited or scared?" asked Flora.

Olivia considered this. "Both," she said finally. "I mean, I can't wait to see the look on Melody's face when she gets the paper back, but —"

"Did you put down wrong answers for the entire assignment?" interrupted Nikki.

"Nope. Not the *entire* assignment. I thought that might make Mr. Krauss suspicious. But the answers are mostly wrong. She'll get a D for sure. And I'm pretty certain I'll get an A, since there was only one problem I had trouble with. Oh, this is going to be great. Melody will be all cocky because as far as she knows, she's come up with the perfect plan. She thinks she's found a way to get the answers to the homework and punish me at the same time. Plus, she thinks I don't have a clue about what she's doing."

"She doesn't know who she's messing with," said Nikki.

"The only thing," Olivia continued, serious again, "is the question of retribution. And that's the part that scares me."

"Yeah," said Flora. "Just how mad will this make Melody?"

"Or will it simply teach her a lesson?" asked Nikki.

Olivia shook her head. "I don't know. But when you think about it, what can Melody do to me? She can't take my friends away — and I have you guys, plus the kids in the book club."

"Including Jacob," said Flora.

Olivia blushed. "Whatever."

"All the teachers really like you," said Nikki. "If Melody did anything truly horrible and you talked to the teachers about it, they'd believe you."

"And now I'm going to get my locker fixed. Or switch to another one," added Olivia.

The girls fell silent.

"Well . . ." said Flora, glancing over her shoulder at the students streaming into Central.

"I wish I didn't have to wait until after lunch," said Olivia. "This is going to be one long day."

By the time math class finally rolled around, Olivia decided she was more excited than afraid. She arrived extra early in order to be able to watch the entire Melody Show.

She wasn't disappointed.

Olivia sat primly at her desk, books piled neatly to the side. She watched her classmates enter the room. Melody was one of the last to arrive, and she sent an insincere grin in Olivia's direction.

Olivia smiled politely back at her.

When everyone was present, Mr. Krauss closed the door to the room, strode to his desk, and picked up a stack of papers. "I have Thursday night's homework for you," he announced. "For the most part, we're making good progress."

Olivia watched as her classmates waited anxiously for Mr. Krauss to hand back the papers. The students looked first at the top of their papers to see the grade written in red ink, then glanced discreetly around the room in an effort to see their friends' grades. Olivia was still trying to decide whether her joke would be more effective if her paper was handed back before or after Melody's, when Mr. Krauss, appearing grim, stopped by Melody's desk. He removed a sheet from the sheaf in his hands.

Olivia strained shamelessly to see the red letter at the top. She had to stop herself from saying, "Why, Melody, you've gotten a D!" And for the first time in her life, she wished mightily that she owned a cell phone camera. How satisfying it would be to take a picture of Melody's face — several pictures, actually — and send the photos to Flora and Nikki. Olivia had to content herself, however, with trying to memorize Melody's various expressions so she could describe them later.

First Olivia saw surprise, complete and utter surprise. This was followed by embarrassment (Melody's face turned a rewarding shade of pink), but the embarrassment soon changed to a smirk. Ha, thought Olivia. Melody thinks I didn't understand the assignment and now *I'm* going to get a D, too. That, she realized, would be just as pleasing to Melody as stealing Olivia's work in order to get an A.

Olivia couldn't help herself. She flashed Melody another smile. Then she waited for Mr. Krauss to approach her desk. In the next moment, he did so, and he handed her a paper bearing a nice fat A. One glance showed Olivia that she hadn't missed a single problem, not even the one that had given her trouble.

Olivia angled the paper so that Melody could see it easily.

"Nice work, Olivia," said Mr. Krauss.

"Thank you," she replied.

"Melody," he continued, "I would like to see you after class."

Olivia allowed herself one final look at Melody, whose expression had turned to a combination of surprise (again) and anger. Then she ignored Melody for the rest of the period. When Olivia left the classroom later, Melody was standing miserably at Mr. Krauss's desk.

In the hallway, Olivia saw, to her own surprise, Flora and Nikki, who were waiting breathlessly to find out what had happened.

"It was fabulous!" Olivia exclaimed softly. "Simply fabulous! You should have seen the look on her face. It was *so* worth everything."

"What was worth everything?" asked Jacob, joining the girls.

"Hey, Olivia! Hey, you guys!" Claudette rounded the corner, followed by Mary Louise and several other members of the book club.

And that was how it happened that when Melody finally left Mr. Krauss's room that day, she found Olivia Walter, smiling and happy, surrounded by a large group of friends, including Jacob.

Melody gathered her face into something resembling a smile. "Hi, everyone!" she said.

"'lo," said Claudette.

Jacob glanced at her. "Hey."

"Um," said Melody, and she edged around the group of kids and disappeared in the crowded hallway.

"The best thing," Flora said to Olivia later that day, "is that no one even knows what Melody did to you, and they *still* can't stand her."

"I have a feeling, though," Olivia replied, "that I'd better get my locker taken care of right away."

"I'll go with you," said Flora, and she put her arm around her friend.

Tuesday, September 30th

Flora was awakened early on Tuesday morning by Ruby, who ran into her room, exclaiming, "Flora! When we get up tomorrow we have to remember to say 'Rabbit, rabbit' first thing."

"And you woke me up to tell me this?" mumbled Flora.

Ruby plopped down on the edge of her sister's bed. "Your alarm's going to go off in five minutes, anyway. You know," she said thoughtfully, "there really ought to be something you say on the last day of each month, too. Why just the first day? I think on the last day you should say, 'Ferret, ferret' or 'Mole, mole.'"

"'Ferret, ferret' or 'mole, mole'?"

"To keep it in the rodent family."

Flora rolled over. After a moment, she said, "I can't believe it's the last day of September."

"Yeah," said Ruby, and she made a smacking noise.

"Are you chewing *gum*?" asked Flora, horrified. "It's not even six-thirty."

Ruby shrugged. Then she said, "So, tomorrow is October, and that means Halloween and then Thanksgiving and then Hanukkah and then Christmas and then Kwanzaa and then New Year's Eve and then Valen —"

"Yeah, yeah, all the holidays," muttered Flora.

"You sure are grouchy."

"Well, don't you remember what else today is? Besides the last day of September?"

"Is it . . . did I forget Min's birthday?" screeched Ruby.

"No! Today is the day Mr. Willet leaves."

Ruby's face fell. "Oh. Right."

Flora stretched and turned on her light. "Maybe it's a good thing you woke me up. We need time to say good-bye to Mr. Willet before we leave for school this morning."

"I know. But, Flora, he *is* only going to be a few miles away."

"It's still going to be sad. I mean, having an empty house in the row. I don't ever remember an empty house here — not even before we moved to Camden Falls."

"Well, somebody new will move in soon," said Ruby. "And that will be kind of exciting. I wonder who it will be. Maybe a family with kids our age."

"Or with a baby so Grace won't be the youngest kid in the row. And Olivia and I will have someone else to baby-sit for."

"Maybe it will be another couple just like Mr. and Mrs. Willet. Well, not *just* like them. I don't want the lady to have Alzheimer's. But you know what I mean." Ruby paused. "Or maybe it will be a family with two teenage boys and Margaret and Lydia will fall in love with them and there will be a double wedding in the backyards."

Flora smiled. "We could be junior bridesmaids."

"Yes!" exclaimed Ruby, imagining her dress.

"But right now we have to get ready to say good-bye to Mr. Willet."

Min accompanied Flora and Ruby to Mr. Willet's house after breakfast. "I might as well say good-bye now, too," she said, "before I leave for the store."

They weren't the only ones there. Every one of the Row House neighbors who would soon be leaving for school or work had planned to drop by Mr. Willet's that morning.

"Oh," said Flora, her lip quivering as Mr. Willet held his front door open. "Look, Ruby. Look, Olivia."

Mr. Willet's living room wasn't empty yet, but it had the look of a house that had lost its owner. Much of the furniture had already been given away, since it wouldn't fit in the apartment at Three Oaks. And the

Willets' belongings had been packed into cartons bearing labels such as BOOKS, KNICKKNACKS, PHOTO ALBUMS, AND ODDS AND ENDS — TO BE UNPACKED LATER.

Mr. Willet was talking to Mr. Morris. "The movers are scheduled to arrive at nine," he was saying.

"Roger and John and I will be over later this afternoon to give you a hand with the unpacking," Mr. Morris replied.

"See?" Ruby said to Flora. "Mr. Willet will still have all his old friends around. Mr. Morris and Dr. Malone and Mr. Edwards are going to help him out today."

Flora nodded. "Min said I can visit on Friday." She looked at her watch. "Well . . . I guess this is it. We'd better say good-bye or we'll be late for school."

Flora and Ruby and Olivia surrounded Mr. Willet and each gave him a hug.

"We'll see you soon," said Olivia.

As Flora walked through the door, she heard Min say behind her, "You've been a wonderful neighbor, Bill. You and Mary Lou are dear friends."

"I can't tell you how much I'm going to miss all of you," replied Mr. Willet.

"But you need to be with Mary Lou again," said Min.

"Yes."

When Flora and Olivia returned from school that afternoon, they paused at the path leading to the house that had been the Willets'.

"Empty," remarked Flora.

"It *feels* empty, doesn't it?" said Olivia. "Even from the outside. I don't know why, since it looks just the same as all the other houses."

"I think houses know when they've been left alone, just like people do."

Flora and Olivia walked on to their own houses. Flora let herself inside. She patted King Comma and hugged Daisy Dear and went to her bed, where she lay down and had a small cry.

CHAPTER 32

October

All across Camden Falls, people have turned the pages of their calendars from September to October. On Main Street the themes of the store windows have changed from back-to-school to Halloween and even Thanksgiving. If you were to walk along a single block, you would see Needle and Thread's display of hand-sewn Halloween costumes, the array of ghost stories in Time and Again, the Halloween baskets in Sincerely Yours, and the spooky lawn decorations in Zack's hardware store. On this Friday evening, you might notice a very excited young man standing outside Zack's. The young man is Robby Edwards, and he's trying to convince his father to buy everything they would need to turn their front yard into a cemetery. "Look!" exclaims Robby. "Skeleton hands and skeleton feet and tombstones. Wouldn't those be perfect for Halloween?"

Leave Main Street behind (Robby and his father are striking a deal in which Robby agrees to pay for some of the decorations out of his salary), and walk through the chilly air to the Row Houses on Aiken Avenue. Darkness is falling and lights are on in all the houses except the second one from the left. If you are very observant, you will notice a small hole in the yard of this house where a FOR SALE sign recently stood.

In the house at the left end of the row, Lacey and Mathias, the Morris twins, are engaged in a conversation their mother fears will soon turn into a fight.

"Guess what," says Lacey. "I'm one month older than I was at the beginning of September."

"Well, I'm one second older than I was at the beginning of this sentence."

"No. That sentence is longer than one second. You're three seconds older than at the beginning of the sentence."

"But it took *you* six seconds to say all that so I'm really —"

"Kids," Mrs. Morris interrupts. "Enough. Come into the kitchen, please. Supper's ready."

Now step away from the Morris house. Three doors down is Min Read's home. On this evening, Min and Ruby are here and so is Mr. Pennington, but Flora is at Three Oaks having dinner with Mr. Willet. Ruby, who returned from her tap class claiming she was absolutely famished, has already eaten her supper and is now tap-tapping away in the front hallway, whispering a new routine under her breath. "And time step, time step, fa-lap, ball-change . . ." In the kitchen, Rudy Pennington and Min sit next to each other on one side of the table, a casserole of chicken and vegetables forgotten on the counter. They're holding hands and talking quietly.

Next door, the Walters will be eating a late dinner. Sincerely Yours stayed open for a special sale this evening, so dinner won't be on the table for a while yet. Olivia, having already helped her father make a salad, has closed herself into her room. Presently, Jack knocks on her door and says, "Olivia! Telephone!" Olivia is surprised. Flora is at Three Oaks, and Olivia just got off the phone with Nikki. Who could be calling now? A shudder runs down her spine — Melody? Has Melody come back to haunt her? She hasn't spoken to Olivia since the day the homework papers were returned, and so far, Olivia's nice, new locker seems to be in working order, but Olivia has a feeling she hasn't heard the end of Melody. Heart pounding, she opens her door and takes the phone from Jack.

"Hello?" she says.

"Hello, Olivia? This is Jacob," the caller replies.

Several miles away, on the outskirts of Camden Falls — at the very moment Jack hands Olivia the telephone — a car pulls into the driveway of Nikki's house. Nikki and Mae and Mrs. Sherman have just sat down to their dinner. They're not expecting a visitor and they look at one another warily. Mrs. Sherman is rising from her chair when the front door bangs open and a man's voice calls, "Hello?"

Mae leaps to her feet. "Tobias! It's Tobias!"

And into the kitchen he strides.

Mrs. Sherman hugs her son. "What a wonderful surprise!" she exclaims.

"How long can you stay?" asks Nikki.

"All weekend," he answers.

"Yes!" cries Mae. "Oh, goody! All weekend. Tobias, look what we taught Paw-Paw to do. We taught him to dance. The trick is named Ballerina. All you need is a dog cookie —"

"Honey, give your brother a chance to catch his breath," says Mrs. Sherman.

Tobias flings his backpack on the floor and joins his family at the table. Nikki fixes him a plate of food.

"Three plus one is four," says Mae with satisfaction.

Back in Camden Falls, several streets from Aiken Avenue, Allie Read is finishing up a day of writing. The afternoon has been particularly productive and she closes her laptop with a snap, looking forward to a quiet evening. In the kitchen, she removes various items from the refrigerator and begins to prepare her dinner. She sets one place at the table. She considers the place. She considers the small meal on the stove. She considers the one umbrella in the stand in the front hall and the mostly empty coatrack nearby. Everything seems somehow insignificant.

Allie sighs. And then she does the thing that she has told herself she must stop doing so often. She climbs the stairs to the second floor, turns on the hall light, opens a closet door, and stands before the closet. She looks over the shelves of baby supplies. After a moment, she selects a tiny yellow shirt, holds it to her cheek, and then returns it to the shelf.

She closes the door on her secret.

Author photo © Dion Ogust

ANN M. MARTIN lives in upstate New York in a town not unlike Camden Falls. She loves to sew and loves to take walks with her dog, Sadie. She also has two cats, Gussie and Woody.

Ann's acclaimed novels include *Belle Teal*, *A Corner of the Universe* (a Newbery Honor), *Here Today*, *A Dog's Life*, and *On Christmas Eve*. Her much-loved series The Baby-sitters Club has sold over 176 million copies since it began.

To find out more about Ann, please visit
www.scholastic.com/mainstreet

Spend some time on

Main Street

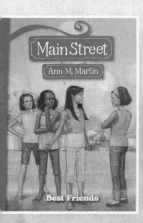

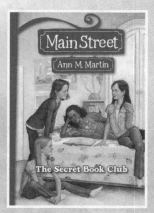

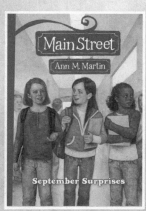

Visit www.scholastic.com/mainstreet

- ○ Explore the interactive map of Camden Falls
- ○ Send a postcard from Main Street
- ○ Download fun scrapbooking activities
- ○ Visit the stores for fun crafts and activities

📖 SCHOLASTIC

MSWEB6

A new girl is moving to Main Street! Will she fit in?

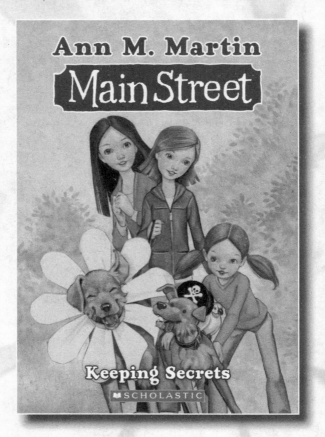

Flora, Ruby, Olivia, and Nikki are excited to meet their new neighbor, Willow. So why doesn't she want to meet them? Does she have something to hide?

Heartland ™

■ SCHOLASTIC

scholastic.com/titles/heartland

HEARTBL

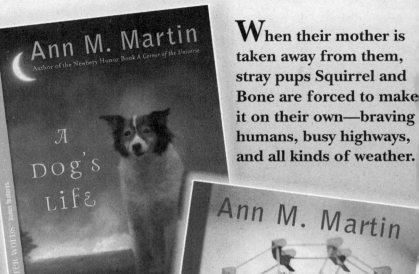